BOOK OF STY II

KRONIKULS *of* STYOPOS J. BUCK

ANDY "CHICO" DAVIS

Book of Sty II
Copyright © 2024 by Andy "Chico" Davis

ISBN: 979-8895311196 (sc)
ISBN: 979-8895311202 (e)

All rights reserved. No part of this publication may be reproduced, distributed, or transmitted in any form or by any means, including photocopying, recording, or other electronic or mechanical methods, without the prior written permission o f the publisher and/or the author, except in the case of brief quotations embodied in critical reviews and other noncommercial uses permitted by copyright law.

The views expressed in this book are solely those of the author and do not necessarily reflect the views of the publisher, and the publisher hereby disclaims any responsibility for them.

Writers' Branding
(877) 608-6550
www.writersbranding.com
media@writersbranding.com

DEDICATION

This small work is dedicated to my beloved Mother.
CARRIE LEE HELAIRE DAVIS
February 3, 1920 - August 13, 2002

Dear Mother/We share "Heartbeats" of each"Other", The moment you passed onto glory//The Almighty ordained an eternal, "Mother and son "Love Story'/Tis Godsend//Shall never end, Mother/Like you, there will never be another/One of a kind/Forever, via "Shared Heartbeats" we eternally, bind/Akin to a "Foxfire", our hearts pulsate/ Yes Mer Dear/, I know you will be the first to greet me, at "Heaven's Gate.'

Eternal Love,

Andrew, Jr

Contents

I. Foreword 1
II. Introduction 3

Days of Grass

1. Madame Carrie Lee 8
2. 16 Scrofers 18
3. 200 Hundred Acres and a Deere 20
4. Da Rage 24
5. Da Cotton Picker 28
6. Da Karmapucka 30
7. Da Clairvoyant 33
8. In Cahoots 37
9. Da Days of my Life 40
10. Hard Times 42
11. Slavery Bridges 44
12. Da Gap 46
13. Silence of the AM 49

Leaves of Nirvana

1. Awakening 56
2. Me-d-da Lord 61
3. Dis Ol Soul Of Mine 65

4. Scriptures/Squalms/Sasa 66
5. Life's Bits-n-Pieces 70
6. Another Day.. 72
7. I Got Today Under My Skin / Get "Tumorrow" From Under My Skin / Yestiddy 74
8. Ripples in da Stream 76
9. Seven-Seven-Eight-O 77
10. Man of Age 79
11. We Come and Go 81
12. Potpourri Mind Slake... 82
13. Leetha Kovid... 84
14. MODIMI 86
15. Across Da Great Beyond.. 87
16. Five Leaf Clover Scrolls 89
17. Idioms Of Styopos J. Buck 93
18. Doggerels 95

FOREWORD

Chico, in reviewing your treasure, "Book of Sty II" from whence comes the odd term, "Kronikuls", nowhere to be found in either English or foreign languages. A longtime friend of ours asked me to pose the question, as to its origin.
Brother Eli, why does the word need to be a dictionary feather. Maybe someday it will make Wikipedia's pool of terms or become "Websterized".

Well, what if I told you that it oozed from da leaking mind of one, Styopos J. Buck/As he lay sprawled atop da bed of his "56 Chevy truck/After being flattened by a grand mal torpedo/Which left his mind at ground zero".
Wait a minute now, who in the heck is Styopos J. Buck?
SJB is my fourth person familial, after Andrew, Andy, Chico, get it?

During the aura swell of recovery, from da grand mal, a voice in my head kept beeping "Sty, legacy articles, legacy articles, urgency, urgency". Upon full recovery, instead of the term, "articles", came "Kronikuls", which will adapt, hopefully, to all fields of "Book of Sty".

So, from carnage of the seizure slugfest, evolved the term "Kronikuls", which landed in the "Book of Sty" literary tool box alongside, metaphors, allegories, similes, and the like.

The book runs the gamut from childhood through the "Septo-Octo Gap", da ten year period between ages seventy and eighty.
At present, I can feel the claws of Father Time, tightening around my neck, creating a pulsating insurgency to leave a legacy trail, no matter how narrow. I have very few sans left in my "Sourglass".
Well Chico, I mean Sty, we are right around the same age, but I'm not worried about no legacy trails. I will leave some on the golf course, if my game improves.
Brother Eli the "sum of all fears", now besets me, and "Kronikuls" afforded opportunities to honor many beloved ones, and expose trials, tribulations of mortals, coming and going,

I think the following definition will "Styipedia", "Kronikuls", Kronikuls,(Obj.) A term, depicting past, present, events, that fracture imagination's prism, and criss-cross standard planes of sanity, insanity, during life' travels, trials, tribulations.

You too much, Chico, you too much. Your flagellated mind is sure to leave a "legurcy" trail. Unique to mankind. I am out.

INTRODUCTION

I am "G", a Phantom of the Author", asked to ferry a few lines of introduction to Book of Sty II, dedicated to our dear mother, one Carrie Lee Helaire-Davis, February 3, 1920 - August 13, 2002.

The author of this work, and I, share "Eyelids of Each Other", even though I passed on to glory, back in time.

The term "Sty", has led to queries to the author, as to its meaning, origin, implication. The word conjures up images of encampment of pigs, as in pig sty.

A friend, who is well aware of his love for classic art, paintings, literature, suggested the term was rued from fascination with the year 1600 work by Brughei, depicting a peasant being pushed into a pig sty.

Others offer that the term stems from deep rooted experiences as a sharecropper's son, and its poverty ridden environment.

Lighthearted teasing erupted when a sibling suggested that he had dropped a letter from the word "Stye", a form of eye infection, in deference to our "Shared Eyelids", annunciation.

The answer to the riddle is rather straightforward by the author, in that "Sty", is the moniker of Styopos J. Buck, whom the author names as his, get this, "fourth person familial".

He suggests that in real time there exist Andrew, Andy, Chico, with Styopos J. Buck, being a combination of all three personalities.

In penning this short narrative, though it might be much to the delight of the author, and say all of the above, encompass the origin of "Sty", and leaves that have fallen from its literary tree.

"Kronikuls, as he puts it, are leaves from his "tree of knowledge", whose roots run deeper than most. Back in time, an entire race of people were shackled, bound, shoved into pig stys, as auction chattel, by slave owners, during dark moments in American history.
I haven't met any of the slavery saboteurs during my sojourn in da Milky Way, my guess is that hell abounds with such heathens.
Once a reader settles into "Book of Sty II", it will become crystal clear that a "Styopos J. Buck", is found in all of us. During my sojourn on planet earth, I was in constant battles with "me", "myself", and "I", won a few, lost many.

In this work, literary guard rails are obfuscated, and one must use all imagination bulbs available.
Metaphors, allegories, similes, are tools of the trade, which allow literary giants, as well as novices, opportunities to leave imprints on minds of the living. Toss into the mix, opinions on racial divides, longevity, destiny, and one gets a potpourri of narratives that stretch from one end of the literary spectrum to the other.
Mer Dear loved to read,which inspired siblings to follow in her footsteps, and led to all eight of us obtaining college degrees...

I am humbled by the author's trust in me, to preface what has been a huge challenge on his part. Book of Sty II, is rooted in life experiences, trials, tribulations. Well beyond the pale..

Constant battles with dragons of destiny, have been unkind, but my brother has been steady as a rock, against all odds. He is still my mentor, soul brother, "Eyelids Sharer" in spirits known only to us.

We had lots of fun together, and will always be birds of a feather. My death brought an abrupt end to a lineage of two souls, a few years apart in age, but always on the same page, family wise. Love of family was our rallying cry, and continues, even though I am no longer a man of the flesh.

An "Almighty Power", is now the keeper of my soul,but our spirits remain as one.

Open your channels of imagination, light candles of inspiration, and let the following "Kronikuls" be wickers that burn infernally in your soul. My "Eyelids" have begun to flutter, this time to dis-enjoin.
Hey bro, Mer Dear, Dad, Elsie Mae, and "G" await our copies of Book of Sty II..
GGD to ACD/ With Love/ From above the Astral Plane. /

DAYS OF GRASS

"MADAME CARRIE LEE"

I have failed many times in attempts to compose a salutation to my dear mother, Carrie Lee. On numerous occasions I struggled in vain in attempts to find words to aptly describe her deeds, beauty, motherhood, and impact on lives of others.

But, I am running out of time, and it would be a downright sin, on my part, if I departed without summoning the will power to scribble a few lines in her honor.

Madame Carrie Lee, rich in spirit, love, scratched her footprints indelibly in sands of time. Tis with utmost respect, when I say, she was one of a kind, wielded heavy discipline hands, but was never an assailant.

Her teachings, beliefs, were steeped in christianity, leading to her being an ardent follower of our Lord and Saviour, Jesus Christ, tugging eight siblings along for the ride.

During our younger days, life was hard, but she taught us how to take the bitter with the sweet, and not carry feelings on our sleeves.

The Bible was her holy grail and she fervently believes in its teachings that mankind reaps what is sown. That truth is a guiding light that rarely dimmers, and serves one well, forever and a day.

With trifle exceptions, mother's beauty, seep beyond skin deep, grows, as sure as the wind blows,

Truth be told//Their love cannot be bought, nor sold/It is boundless/ Almighty God, is their witness,

I weep for my Mother, Carrie Lee/ She is dead/But yet, crystal clear images of her, dance in my head/Each day, I bow to her on bending knee/ Eternal love keeps us cheek to cheek/Into her eyes, I peek,

My Imagination runs wild/Back to the days, I sat on her lap as a child/ At times I was her lil boy blue/As she rocked me back and forth in front of fire from da chimney flue/ On others, a man child/Strong, akin to feared animals of the wild/Humble/But yet ready to rumble,
Madame Carrie Lee/You are my spiritual firmament/Reincarnation lent/ My eternal life apogee.

"Mother", you deserved so much more out of life/But, not once did you complain about its toils and strife/You taught we siblings how to take bitter pills of life, with da sweet/Be strong as frozen leather, tough, always stand on our own two feet,

We eight siblings were gathered around a campfire the other night, and truths about your life, its tools of motherhood, strife, glory, were spun, with reverence and delight,
We couldn't stop commenting on the legendary "Sweat Spot", that would swell on the tip of your nose when you were angered, under the collar hot. During such times all stayed out of your way. But that was okay because we all knew how hard times affected the entire clan.

Once we got to talking about the biscuits you used to bake, our love for you spiked to another level. We boys mocked your daughters, on their inability to challenge your mastery of kneading dough.
We reminisced on how Dad coveted the biscuits in the corners of the pan, and was always honored as first person served. We couldn't stop laughing at how I tried to be a prima donna, and get the biscuits from the middle of the pan, in that they were the juiciest.
Other wives, relatives, friends, played second fiddle, when it came to cooking, baking,because you were the cream of da crop.
We got a kick out of talking about how you provided escapes from da cotton, corn fields, no matter what, when it came to your favorite daytime radio programs. We dropped da hoes,cotton sacks, made it home in time for you to catch "Our Gal Sunday", on the radio. which you followed religiously,

I got tremendous joy out of watching you cook, as you listened to your favorite music, with sheer delight.

Our radio was a staple in our abode, and eased the pain, drudgery, of back breaking labor in the fields. A television set came much later, and was a complete joy.

Gun Smoke, Grand old Opry, Jack Benny, Amos-n-Andy, Uncle Remus, Brooklyn Dodger baseball, Joe Louis boxing, to name a few, filled a lot of holes during turbulent times in our lives.

I am still amazed by your ability to raise eight kids, aid relatives, friends, in-laws, on meager earnings from sharecropping and other poverty laden means of survival. Our old country home was like a revolving door, always open to folks in need,not once did you turn anyone away. In reality, you were the "Village Angel", with a heart of gold. How you stretched the commodities, garden foods to feed us and others, goes beyond description. But, I understand now that when we help others, we help ourselves.. People gravitated towards your kindness in groves in your role as "Village Angel".

Mother, did you recognize the fact that the the area of our house, we considered to be the front, was actually the back end. The kitchen sat in the so called front area,while the porch was in the so called rear. The front of our home faced Cane River. I guess it was confusing because of the gravel road that bisected the house and fields. The mailbox, Rte Box 27, was also located along the gravel road.

Looking back, isn't it amazing how that lone gravel road connected us to the rest of the world. The postman, school bus, teachers, visitors, strangers, white bosses all had one avenue, Cane River Road.

The road truly was well constructed, riveted by ditches on either side, and even had a large barrel like , tin opening that served as a channel and dumped overflow rain into Cane River, remarkable.

Meager earnings were always at the forefront but you had ways of making us feel we were the richest folks on earth. Everybody was better off from your generosity.

We found joy in family trips to visit relatives on weekends, holidays. Somehow, several bodies were jammed into the Oldsmobile, and we had jolly good times during trips to visit family, friends...
During the long drive many tales were told by Dad, on his ability to shoot marbles, win money during his heydays, as we traveled, laughing all the way, along the highways and byways.
The trips to see Grandma Emily are cherished most. You two were so much alike, and she would just light up at the sight of us. You all were like two peas in a pod.

Grandma's baked sweet potatoes, cornbread, collard greens were delicious., not to mention the mouth watering apple pies, you two would bake, from time to time.

Uncle Willie was the family entertainer and had the Victrola ready when we arrived. He loved to put the old 78 records on, and crank up music of all types, with down home blues, leading the way.
"Swing Low, Sweet Chariot", was your favorite, and we took delight in humming lyrics along with you.

The family baseball games we played in the cow pasture, adjacent to Aunt Emma Lee's house, were awesome.. I hit a few homers in my day, as you watched from afar, with sheer delight.

During somber times, I recall the latter stages of your life, after dad passed, and the little things that meant a lot to you.. Reading the bible, grandkids, church, choir practice, head the list.
Planted in my mind are images of the many times I journeyed home on weekends, and found you sitting in front of the television set, alone.
During those times we were very much in need of each other. I was at the crossroads of life, and had no inkling as to what road I wished to travel. You gave me direction and hope.

I am forever grateful for your mental toughness, which you used to teach siblings how to rebuff arrows of high crimes and misdemeanors. That unique quality, power, saved our family from being split asunder, by sins of the world.

Your unwavering faith in God, planted seeds in we siblings, that sprout forever and a day. Your undying loyalty to church duties, unmatched Your spiritual support for Dad, during his final days, was something to behold. Not once did you leave his bedside, during his entire stay at the hospital, epitomizing a loyal wife until he passed away quietly in his sleep.

The humane things you did for others, taught lessons, rules, to follow. One being, "Do unto others, as you would have them do unto you". Wouldn't the world be a better place to live, if we adhered to such a simple principle. A lot has transpired since your death. We have lost two precious siblings, one brother, one sister, and a host of relatives, friends.. I forgot, you probably know already, since you now share the same kingdom, with those fortunate enough to reach the land of milk-n-honey.

The world is currently trapped in the throes of a horrific virus pandemic, and death tolls are unimaginable. Your baby sister passed recently and is heaven bound to join you, on heaven's shore..

Time is no longer on my side, and every day is now stoked with urgency. A lifetime has proven to be just a lightning flash in a pan. No matter how hard I try, I cannot hold back the hands of Father Time.

At times, I feel as though I've been a complete failure and have not lived up to your expectations. I dare not ask, where have all the flowers gone.

I'd rather have one more day with you, than all the tea in China, as the saying goes. We would revisit people, places, things, which brought you pure joy.
A fishing trip, up Cane River, would be first priority, and I would make sure the fish were biting so you would catch your fill of "Red Horses". Red

Horse is the name we ascribed to the big trout fishes, due to their rainbow like colors. Fried fish must surely be served in heaven.
After catching our fill,I would have a surplus of fine ingredients, needed to mix and bake pans of your legendary biscuits, cornbread.. My mouth waters, from just the thought of such an experience.

Nostalgia driven thoughts of honey, Steen syrup, milk from ol Lula (our cow angel), biscuits, bacon, ham, sausages, hominy grits, eggs, set my soul on fire. I sorely miss the fun filled times at the breakfast table, come what will, come what may,

Next up would be a shopping spree at Nichols Department Store, to purchase the finest of finest, shoes, dresses, hats, shawls, in preparation for our outings at church, Nussy's Café and ballroom. At Nussy's, John Lee Rooker, and his band, will be there to provide the music. We will "Two-Step", the night away. I might pluck a few tunes on my guitar, to surprise you.
At church, it was arranged for us to be a duet,and sing the full version of "Swing Low, Sweet Chariot". Additionally, we will place wreaths on grave sites, yours, Dad's, Glenn's, Elsie, and other family members who have passed on to glory.

The family dinner at Shane Soul Food Restaurant, will include your favorites.. pork chops, red beans-n- rice, mashed potatoes, mustards, string beans, yams, prime steaks, roasts, fried chicken, fish,gumbo, shrimps, oysters, clam chowder soup, cornbread, biscuits, and if you so desire,chitterlings. Your choice of apple pie, lemon meringue, strawberry shortcake, vanilla ice cream, and the family favorite, pecan pie. Oh, I almost forgot, lemonade, your all time favorite drink..

Dad, Uncle Hue, Glenn, Elsie, grandpas, grandmas, aunts, uncles, will all be present, even If I have to dig them up out of their graves.

"Mer Dear", do you recall how my siblings used to poke fun at my disdain for tripe, chitterlings, rabbit, squirrel, opossum, meals. The same holds true today.

But It was a different story when it came to duck, deer, steak, chicken, fish, leftovers from parties at the local Country Club. We gathered the scrapings as we mopped, cleaned the joint on Sunday evenings, after the partying was over by the rich folks. What a difference in lifestyles, eats, A fireside chat will crown your stay. While munching on roasted sweet potatoes, we will reminisce, and travel down nostalgia's alley.
I will be sure to recall the memorable times you and your lady friends spent "Quilting". We boys would end up in near fights doting on which lady was the best "Quilter", you got my vote every time.

I promise not to discuss my childhood, and the many illness bridges you carried me across.

Mer Dear, there were many times, when thoughts of suicide burdened me. . Such omens came to the forefront, after your brother, Uncle Huey drowned at an early age.. His death was due to an epileptic seizure, while middling around the edge of Cane River. Little did I know that later in life I would become a "Seizureplectic',
It would have been best if I had just dove into the muddy waters, trying to save him and never come up.

Recently, we found a photo of you as a nursemaid for a wealthy caucasian family. You appeared to be around nine or ten years old, and we siblings couldn't decide whether or not to seethe with anger, rip it apart, or cherish the past.. We finally agreed to encircle the photo in a gold frame, I am so happy we did. I can't imagine what it must've been like to sleep on the ground underneath the masters mansion, as you once described it.

Images of racism's ropes, poverty 's chains, raise their ugly heads, each time I look at the picture of you with the Caucasian family, but such was better than you pulling a cotton sack.
Despite the cruelty of it all, not once did we hear you complain about the wretchedness of life . "Mer Dear", would you believe it, if I told you that racism's ropes, poverty's chains, are still still hanging, clanging, today. Well, they are, just in a more sophisticated manner. The more things change, the more they remain the same.

Mer Dear, "Madame Carrie Lee"/Death doth not do us part/You are my eternal flame, spiritual apogee/My lifeblood, ever throbbing,, "Second Heart",

I stare at a picture of us,cheek to cheek/Into your beautiful eyes, I peek/ My "Second Heart", is beating fast/Forever, I wish the moment could last/ Imagination, sends me down a long, winding alley/I peck along on my walking cane/Determined to reach Resurrection Valley/Once there, I will meet/Greet/You, my spiritual angel, "Carrie Lee"/Beneath da idyllic, apple tree,
Dear Mother, Carrie Lee/ Hope you enjoyed our reincarnation, jubilee/ Sparked by heaven sent rays, as we followed the west to east rising sun/ Towards da Astral Plane, across which, all God's angels run,

Thanks to you, Madame Carrie Lee/My "Second Heart" runs free/Has powers to mutate/Reincarnate/Affording me spiritual energy /Astral Plane synergy/So, I'm going to be quite contrary/Celebrate your 102nd birthday, the entire month of February/ Bring along all siblings, off-springs/Dance on cloud nine, with one Madame Carrie Lee, "Our Angel of Rings'.

Well, Mer Dear, tis time to say good bye, I am really struggling during this moment in time. My world is empty, seemingly void of purpose, as I drift through my overtime period of life. having used up all yellow, red, flags, timeouts, but I continue to toot my metal pea whistle ferociously on what I have so named "TwoDay".
On "TwoDay", I try to live twice as fast as I do on others. This gives me a feeling of elaboration and puts me in tunes with the awesome sound of nature's creatures. Sounds from humming birds, bumble bees, flutters of butterfly wings, hoot owls, and the like, drown out the Tinnitus Ramblings in my head.

Travails of the SARS pandemic have taken much joy out of everyday existence. I had my time in its circular firing squad ring, and believe me , "Mer Dear" staring in the eyes of death offers no flash points.

Prior to our final goodbyes, hugs ,there is one bothersome apology I need to get off my chest. You have my sincere apology for assisting in taking you away from your beloved residence during your final days on mother earth.

Rather than gathering at your bedside in a faraway hospital, your bedroom at our family home should have been the site of your final awakening.

Please forgive all of us, but we were clinging to any hope of survival and couldn't let go of our "Angel".

Keep the other family members in line who have departed, as their "Guardian Angel".

Mother, your love for reading inspired eight siblings to follow in your footpaths. Your third grade education far out distances the higher degrees we achieved. You garnered PHD's in common sense, love for humanity via a mindset that was absolutely brilliant.
O i will close with a small poem for your keepsake during times when you are not imbibing words of "Milk and Honey", from your Lord and Saviour, Jesus Christ.

Our Eternal Love Story

Mother, Mother/We share "Heartbeats" of each other/Commencing da moment you passed on to glory/When da Almighty ordained our mother and son, eternal Love Story,
I shall always treasure da date/Da double "Heartbeats" started pounding in my chest /I became your spiritual "Soulmate/My soul became our "love nest', Our shared double "Heartbeats" are pure joy/Evoking memories of you holding me in your arms as a sickly young boy/Time stands still/Vivid images of you,

Mer Dear, you left a plethora of love currents behind/Electric like currents that ignite family ties that bind/No sibling rivalry/Attributable to your formidable chivalry,

Mer Dear/Images of you remain crystal clear//Oh, they shine so bright/ Like the halo that encircled your head on your last goodnight,

Our shared "Heartbeats" roll into your being my earth angel of perfection/ Queen of each predilection/Da flowers in my field of dreams/I bask in your heaven sent love streams,

I weep for my Mother, she is gone/At times I turn to stone/Blessedly i can turn to our shared Heartbeats/To survive many of life's brutal defeats,

On the glorious grounds of Heaven/I am hoping that there is a Milk-n-Honey "7 Eleven"/ Where you might purchase a winning lottery ticket/ With God's graces,mold a Reincarnation Thicket/A mecca where souls of the living, non living congregate/Meditate/Our shared "Heartbeats" would link us together/With love ties strong as frozen leather,

Well Madame Carrie Lee/Tis time for "Imagination Day" beneath my flowery apple tree/Where i tap my feet with joy in rhythm with our "Shared Double Heartbeats"/I hope to have many more prior to hanging up my life on earth, reincarnation cleats.

With Eternal Love/Andrew, Jr.

"16 SCROFERS"

SCROFERS, "Sharecropper Row of Famers". Name ascribed to individuals tied to America's soils of inequality.

The following words of praise are ascribed to two brothers, who lived side by side, farming lands owned by others. This method of survival is steeped in America's folklore, and is known as "Sharecropping". From this band of brothers came sixteen siblings of different sorts, as each rolled eight kids each, the hard way.

Nine boys, seven girls/ Some with nappy hair, others with golden curls/ Some big, tall/Others skinny, small/Pigmented, black,yellow, brown/ Nary a one, with da same frown /But in sunshine or stormy weather/We "SCROFERS", our bond, always strong as frozen leather,

We forever be, proud siblings of hard working sharecroppers/At times, genteel rich, other dirt poor/But, never imbibed slop from poverty's hoppers/Nor slept on mildew laden floor/Times were hard on the east side of the railroad tracks/But we kept winds from heaven on our backs,

We imbibed our share of coffee-and-bread/Shards of Steen's syrup, like lead// But we vowed to never beg, borrow, nor steal/Mamas, papas, found ways to provide da family meal,

We "SCROFERS", left behind hard days of pulling cotton sacks/ Stooping, bending with aching backs//Long since gone, sitting front row on a church pew/Questioning grandpa's revelations bout da chosen few//Sorely missed are after church meals, games/Blasting each others nick names/Those were times, my friend/Thought they would never end,

We are now scattered all over America's heartland/But forever members of the "Davis- Bobb", genetic strand/ Ancestral ties that bind/Never left behind,/As birds of a feather/We will forever, flock together,

As our numbers dwindle/Ever closer ties we must kindle/Each remains "SCROFER" clone//Love of family, must continue to be etched in stone,

Well, that's about all I have to say, about dem days up Cane River, on the two hundred acre farm. Those were moments in time that left scars on many faces that will never heal. Though times change, in many ways they remain the same. Truthfully speaking, life winds down too quickly, forfeiting extended brushes with the past.

"SCROFERS", Sharecropper Row of Famers, currently there are only two inductees, my dad and uncle, but there are many more to come . My hometown awaits the arrival of my dream of turning a certain street into a marvel that will rival the one in Hollywood

"16 SCROFERS"/ All proud as red breasted rooster/Let's not forget our past/Where Davis-Bobb genetic dye was cast/Continue to stick together/ Akin to birds of a feather,

Faster than an Easter bunny, years slip away/Can't hold back a single day/ Da sharecropping days are gone/But memories of them are etched in stone.

"200 HUNDRED ACRES AND A DEERE"

I am the son of a southern sharecropper, who survived morbid thorns, thistles of segregation, slavery, and poverty.
As a family, we were poor, dirt poor, but were proud as peacocks in spirit.. Found ways to survive under conditions, which put sores on America's face that will never heal.
King Cotton, ruled by land, plowed by human beings, looked upon as mere chattel by plantation owners. It was common for sharecroppers to plant, toil da fields, and end up in the red, void of any avenues of protest. The winter months were brutal, leading to many days of abject hunger and pestilence. But no n matter the consequence, we had "Two Hundred Acres and a Deere" as tree limbs of hope, that might bend, but never break

Sounds of our reliable, green, yellow speckled, John Deere tractor, ring in my ears akin to those of a symphony.

Looking back over the years, brings deeper appreciation for men, women, who found ways to feed, raise large families, under extreme conditions, that brought many to their knees.
I am one of eight siblings, and had a front row seat at poverty's picture show. Being the oldest male sibling, put me at the forefront of what it took to survive, during brutal cold winters that laid souls bare.
But no matter what, no matter how bad things worsened, you always had a "Deere" as a John, for the ages.

During fretful periods of remorse, I have to fight mightily to change course, and not let sins of the past strip me naked, foregoing joys of the present. My soul is forever flooded by anger pods, volatile, akin to lightning rods, whenever images of long ago poverty charades, take on bleak, racial discrimination, shades.

Long vegetate, America's roots of racial discrimination, they run as deep as da Nile. I have not been able to cull a single root of hypocrisy, from America's cotton fields of racial bigotry.

Trials as a sharecropper, its caustic dyes leave indelible stains on the mind, body, and soul.

Da back breaking labor, productivity of sharecroppers, helped make this land of ours, what it is today. Picking cotton, hustling bales to gin mills, threaded da expensive quilts of rich land owners.

Images of their arrogance, and aversion of equality, roll into lifelong distrust of the constitution, itself.
"We hold these truths to be self evident, that all men are created equal, and have the right to equal protection under laws of democracy, did not apply to those with cotton sacks strapped on their backs, or with hoes in their roughened palms.
The law of the land", whichever the saying goes, definitely was not applicable to inhumane treatment of lowly sharecroppers and like neighbors.

Figments, pigments, of poverty's wretchedness, which over time enlarge, paint the souls of so many of us, red, will forever endure. My disdain for da sack, cotton rows, flows, in every crack of my wounded spirit.

For ages, it seems as though I was buried in slavery sands, and I still recoil from images of a cotton picker under the red hot sun. If it weren't for you John my "Deere", we never would have reaped anything we sowed.. Pulling that gray-n-red cotton sack/ Heavy laden, pluck, pluck, pluck/ At times, waddling like a duck/Lleft a lifelong crook in my back. Just last night I had a dream of picking cotton/One that I would rather not save/ Best forgotten/ Whereby I dropped my sack in a steaming cotton row and screamed, "I much rather be buried in my grave."

I am a proud son of a sharecropper, charged with helping in taking care of da brood, putting vittles in da hopper and cultivating the crops with the Deere.
After seven decades, I can still hear the early morning horn that awakened me, to kick start the day. Oftentimes it was chillingly cold, but when I got dressed, I would encounter mother feeding chips of wood to the stove, sipping a cup of coffee.

We would give each other a hug, I would then grab a biscuit, and head for the hay barn, siblings still fast asleep,

Near the barn, awaited ol Lula, Brimmer, our beloved cows mooing in the early morning clear..
Our faithful milk cows, delicate tits, provided rudiments that were musts for preparing family meals. NO milk, no biscuits, cornbread,cream, butter, the list goes on.

Milking a cow, ain't no joke, no okie doke, one must be kind, gentle, when squeezing the tits, to avoid getting kicked in da face. Also, a rapport must be established between da milker and da cow, to get maximum results. Oh Lula, Brimmer, we became birds of a feather.

My dad sharecropped two hundred acres, along with his older brother, each sired eight siblings, later dubbed, "Da Sweet Sixteen". The two were alike, but different in ways that helped both.
Our abode was an all wood, six room shack, void of all modern day heating, lighting, plumbing. Nevertheless, it was kept spotless as the butt of a newborn nursing babe by all of us..

To make a long story, short, I will leave you with the following attempt at literary prose, favoring, "200 Hundred Acres and a Deere".

"Looking back over da years/Evokes anger, laughter, tears/Personifies plights of "Da Sharecropper"/In its quest to keep full its spiritual hopper, Prejudice fueled racial climes/Yielded inhumane, hard times/ Outposts for hunger, degradation/Were barriers to fruitful means of higher education, But to, America, da sharecropper, was a major factor/Due to access to da "John Deere" tractor/Which leveled the playing fields/As da sharecropper found means, ways to experience monetary yields,
We had da Deere and 200 acres of soil/No matter under unfair conditions we had to toil/Suck inequality juices from da landowner's funnel/There was always light at da end of the tunnel,
There was Cane River/Our survival quiver/Arrowhead of trout, bass, catfish/Our means, ways of food dish after dish,

Need to cleanse da body, whim/ Jump in da river,, bathe, swim/Hungry, da watermelon patch/Taste, soul scratch/Sweet potato mound/Taters buried in da ground,
Da "Outhouse"/Much needed, but, watch out for da fecal mouse/ Cotton, corn patches/Love, hate, mismatches,
Cereal milk, sometimes twice used/Never wasted, abused
Our green colored, Oldsmobile car/Forever a family star /Brought much joy, happiness/ God bless,
Shooting marbles underneath da China ball tree/No match for such glee/Can still see that "lag line'/A marble shooter's gold mine/Shot right or left handed/But never grandstanded/Cardinal sin/Around a marble shooting bin,
Brooklyn Dodgers versus da hated Yankees/Immeasurable in disappointment, spiritual, degrees,
Friday night lights/'Saturday night fights/Means of escape from labors of da fields/Sprung forth massive spiritual yields,
Sports, sports/Lifeblood of all kinds, sorts,
Bethel School/A blessing, never an education drowning pool/Taught the ABC's of life, /Toils and strife/Hmm, was the spelling bee champion/The winner, "Antidisestablishmentarianism", still my braggart zion,
Saint Paul Baptist Church/Grandfather's country steeple/My every other Sunday, prayer perch/Alongside ordinary, forever faithful, everyday people, Baptisms/ Spiritual schisms/Communion/Bread, wine, spiritual unionTime with the Lord/Tempered racial discord Me,

"200 Hundred Acres and da Deere", my "John", for da ages, will never be able to turn all its pages,
I have run a long ways, from da cotton fields back home, but I can still hear muffled sounds of da John Deere", moos of da cows,ol Lula, Brimmer,rumblings of Cane River, all stashed in my memory quiver.
Thoughts on the succulent sweetness of my momma's biscuits., enliven my taste buds more so today than yesteryear..

"Son of a Sharecropper, then and now/"John Deere", cultivator of America's soils/Eliminator of many of my spoils/You're forever my "40 Acres Mule and Plow."

DA "JOHNSON GRASS" RAGE

As the son of a former sharecropper, for years I've had a bone to pick, with former hired hands my dad employed to cull out Johnson grass on cotton rows.
Johnson grass impeded production of fertile crops due to the rate their roots multiplied after rains .
Johnson Grass is very hard to control, and that problem is enlarged for sharecroppers, when "hoers", for lack of a better word,. do not cull out their roots,
Da "Johnson Grass" sprouts again during seasonal rain, here come da "hoers", or should I say hired workers,, to service the very same cotton rows, taking away most of the thin profits of da sharecropper.

I was charged with hauling the hired hands, so I got to know them pretty well. They were sly, cunning, and purposely refused to dig out da "Johnson Grass" roots, because they were in cahoots". A truth I realized after my dad abandoned sharecropping.
Images of hired hands, nipping "Johnson Grass" roots, its dew filled leaves, shining in the early morning sun, have enraged me, long after we put away Da Deere, mule, plow.
I am an old man now, retired, and "Johnson Grass" revenge is still on my bucket list.
So, I fire up my 1985 Mercedes Benz Turbo Diesel, and head down south, to seek my revenge. I arrive in my old hometown, and learn that many of the former hired hands, my dad's faithfully employed, have moved to the city, and occupy what is called "Da Bottoms".
I check into a sleazy hotel, on Musalett Street with my list of former hired hands and Jatling gun in tow. Here I am now, near the end of life's rope, struggling to quieten lifelong demons. Day after day, I slide deeper into Alzymus tunnel, the infamous environment where dementia gods proliferate.

I arise this fog laden morning in a rage, feeling like a rabid canine unleashed from a cage with intentions of creating carnage, in mass proportions.

Secretely, I seek the type generated by suicide bombers, serial killers, mass murderers, that will land me on the front page of the local newspaper, the "Cane River Daily Times".

I dress, snatch my Jatling gun off the shelf, scurry outside, race up and down Musalett Street, determined to fire rounds at every former hired hand encountered,
I recognize the main culprits who were in cahoots, who refused to to dig "Johnson Grass" roots. They are now, old, broken down grandpa's, grandma's, ex classmates,
Strangely, I am immune to feelings of any sorts. But, ust before bullets start flying, and cotton chopper changelings start to run, all afraid of dying, and I keep screaming "ain't no need to run/You can't out speed bullets from my Jatling gun", aim, get ready to fire, a strange thing occurs. An elderly lady in red screams," I ain't no former hired hand, karmapucka, I am a dyed in wool, country gal, a "Kornhuska", yo first girlfriend. Mae Lee Bell, can't you tell, by my sumptuous, distinct, smell.
We were teenage lovers, even though stolen perfume from my mama, smelt like morning dew on "Johnson Grass, you didn't mind, let it pass,

I put my revolver on hold, scream, "Mae Lee", you caused my memory patches from the past, to grow thicker, you brought much joy to this cotton picker, c'mon over here, and give me a hug.

Wow, I smell ya, you're still wearing that Lady of Paradise perfume, that smells like dew on "Johnson Grass".
Your perfume scent has abated my rage. Do you remember how we used to talk about my dad's hired hands, not culling out "Johnson Grass" roots, and how after seasonal rain, they were back again.
I watched as it grew, had no idea, the hired hands were in cahoots, ' because they planned, to never chop da "Johnson Grass" roots,

Mae Lee, you sweet smelling "Kornhuska, you came along at the right time, luckily, I have not zinged a former hired hand, cotton chopper, "Karma Pucka", and haven't committed a single crime.' Da dementia gods have taken control of my mind, flipping me backwards, into the past,

where my anger pods never die.' Last night, I could've sworn my salad was littered with "Johnson Grass", it was morass, crass. imbibe, decided to pass.' Suddenly, I stand face to face, with hired hands swinging hoes, screaming, we weren't always gonna be cotton chopping, John Does, we were in cahoots, we never intended to cull da "Johnson Grass", roots.
We knew, come seasonal rain, da "Johnson Grass" would be in full bloom again. We gits da chance to do it all over again, yo daddy's money, cured a lot of poverty, gloom,

I hear police sirens blaring, I stand in the middle of a street staring, down barrels of police rifles, my sense of awareness, dementia gods stifle. A helicopter circles overhead, I whisper to myself, "these trigger happy, karmapucking officers, are anxious to fill my ass full of lead." A voice, on a loudspeaker, from a helicopter bellows. "Put down your gun, turn and face the west to east rising sun. I get down on my knees, my head is buzzing, I feel as though I am amidst a swarm of bumble bees. After all the commotion, fanfare, and an officer approaches, I feel like the lowest of roaches.
Da officer whispers, "sir, you been running up and down da street in da nude, screaming, I'm gonna shoot every former hired hand, cotton chopper I meet, run karmapuckas', run, but you can't out speed bullets from my Jatling gun,
I retort, officer, I have not been firing no gun, I have been trying to grab rays from da west to east rising sun, here take my gun,
I want to use da rays to kill da "Johnson Grass" roots, dem hired hands, cotton chopper karmapuckas," are still in cahoots. They are awaiting seasonal rain, which will cause da "Johnson Grass" to sprout again.
Sir, you ain't down south, you ain't in no place called da "Bottoms", there ain't no Mae Lee Bell, you in da City of Angels, ain't no Johnson grass gonna grow on an asphalt farm, dementia gods have you in their back to da past swarm.
You out here on Jephosat Street, in da nude, with a bad ass attitude. There ain't no lady in red, stoked with Lady of Paradise perfume, that smells like morning dew on "Johnson Grass".
You go on home now, maybe you can eat some "Modu Grass" salad, to abate yo rage, you came very close to being wiped out, by a police rampage,

I keep whispering, "Johnson Grass", you da cause of my lifelong anger, you keep me in clear, unpleasant, danger.
Former hired hands cotton chopper, karmapuckas, you better cull up dem roots, because me -n- da police, are now in cahoots.

I sit on the side of my bed, shaking my head back and forth.
Lately, dreams, nightmares, have been centered around days as a sharecropper's son, and all evils attached to being poor, last night's dream's, prime example. I cringe when images of my mother, dad, trying to make ends meet,during brutal winter seasons, pop into my mind.. Many times I opened the "Ice Box", and found it bare of food.
Scarcity of food, barriers to, health care, education, during that era, were yokes that tightened with each passing year.. I am a prime example of how blacks were used as guinea pigs, especially at Charity hospitals. The suffrages, after effects, are monumental, often lasting, causing unrelenting bitterness..
For many any chances of happiness in life, were left on an operating table, at a charity hospital, manned by butchers, parading as physicians. I was eleven years old, spent what seemed like an eternity in a cold, darkened, hospital room
Childhood wounds have ways of emboldening themselves, in one's mind. in that many are life changing, brutal.
I rise up off the side of my bed, stroll outside and am greeted by a sun filled day.. Westward the sky is lucid and i can see snow caps atop the San Gabriel Mountains.
My flower beds are in dire need of grass culling, so I grass a hoe, chop a few weeds, determined to git dem roots.
I say to myself, "America itself, mirrors a patch of Johnson grass,, and no one yet. has been able to cull out its racial discrimination roots, we all in cahoots.

DA COTTON PICKER

"Da Cotton Sack"/For fifteen years, slung it around my neck/Procuring poverty scars, speck after speck/Tagged me with a life long, bent back, Was merely a human mule/Hog tied.by white man's rule/Few avenues of escape/Heavy was the cotton sack cape,
Da Cotton Sack/Splattered, red and gray/Changed colors throughout the day/ Rued by sweat from the human mule's back,
Shuck, shuck/Pluck, pluck/I could never master the art of filling a cotton sack/No matter how many times I bent my back,
A man's masculinity, was tied to the pounds in his sack/I was always at the bottom of the pack/No matter how I tried/ The weighting scales never lied,

For proof of cotton picking masculinity/I had no affinity/I picked two hundred, three hundred pounds/ I can still hear the braggart sounds,
Grown men, young boys, girls,`patted their chests in my face/ Strangely, I am yet to feel a tinge of disgrace /Got branded as not having "picker's pride/Never broke stride,
Did not bow to humiliation hounds/Derogatory lashes about lack of pounds plucked in a day/I just went merrily on my way,
In fact, had far more important things in mind/Not of the cotton picking kind./Main goal, how to separate from the pack/Get the darn cotton sack off my back.
Pulling a cotton sack ain't no joke/Filling one full of the white stuff, no okie doke/Each takes a toll/With every pluck of a cotton boll,

So, there I was one Friday evening, the sun was going down/Casting, its usual frown/My cotton sack was light/No field overseer in sight
With extreme danger, decided to flirt/To my sack add a few rotten bolls, and red clay dirt,
I winked my eyes at a few suspicious males/As I made my way to the weighting scales,The overseer screamed," a record, in one cotton sack, one hundred twenty six pounds"/Oohs, aahs from cotton pickers were the sounds/I grabbed my four dollars and started to run/Towards the west to east setting sun,

Waited, waitted, no discussions/Repercussions/Surfaced surrounding my feat/ That I had nary an intention of trying to repeat/Learned that the overseer didn't care one iota/Keep job, meet masters daily pound, quota.

Will forever have visions of the cotton sack/Early morn, strapping it on my back/The late Friday evening escapade/No matter the rotten bolls, clay.,that forever enjoined me in the cotton pickers' cavalcade.

"DA KARMAPUCKA"

Styopos J. Buck, this is Yoyo Conshunse, speaking/I'm afraid yo mind is leaking/Needs tweaking/Cause you is freaking/Out, since you dear brutha passed/I is gassed,
Trying to be yo guide/As you continue to slide/ Farther, farther away from reality/At times, I am victim of yo malicious brutality/ You have become a mean "Karmapucka" of sorts/In yo mind sanity, insanity aborts,
Tsi dangerous where I supplicate in yo inflamed brain/Where acidic nitroglycerin leaves an indelible stain/You have become a source of consternation/I have lost complete control of your strings of imagination,
You've become a total stranger/Bubbling with unrestrained anger/Toting sticks of dynamite in yo revenge quivva/Concocted from gangrene waste of yo livva.

You are not to blame for your brutha's passing/ Can't figure out why you are secretly planning on gassing/ Da neighborhood church on da corner of Pavie and Amulet/ Isn't that a catastrophe we'll regret,
You just came off a rampage/A discombobulated inspired rage/One in which you took yo "Zooiville Thugger" baseball bat and demolished yo two television screens/ Smashed them into smithereens/When you switched to a religious channel by accident/Caught the tail end of a hypocrisy sermon which caused you to vent/All yo pent up frustrations /Volatile causations/Ignited by megastar preacher sermon lies./Espousing that only God determines when one dies/When we all know Lady Luck stands her ground/Plays a huge role in bulging, mortality's impound.

Yoyo, you labeled me a "Karmapucka" lurch/Because, there have been times I sat in church/Dispelling lie after lie/About who calls da shot, when time comes for one to die,
That only God speeds/When its one's time to choke on mortality weeds/ Bush, a small blood clot/Can kill a mortal on da spot/Heart attack/Zip, put da mortal in a sack,
A normal, accidental for that matter, death lightning rod /Ain't flashed by God/Many,many times, Lady Luck/Is behind da wheel, steering mortality's truck,

Karmapuckas more or less, control their own fate/Need to stop blaming da Almighty, for setting one's departure date.

Explain, preacher man/if you can/Why Willie da Hobo has reached age ninety nine/Though drunk everyday on muscatel wine/Hasn't seen da inside of a church for over sixty nine years/Of death, has no fears/ Has recovered from six strokes/Three packs of Camels per day, he smokes/All exercises/He despises,
Yoyo, contrast him with a God fearing man/Who every Sunday, dumps his last penny into da tithes pan/Dies of a stroke while running in da church's fundraising marathon/To raise funds to pay for a heart transplant for da nun, Mary Sue Carrollton.

Yes, I'm a bewildered "Karmapucka" who snort/Each time images of my dear brutha, abort/Yoyo, tis best to enjoy da rides on my mind's see saw/ Because my brain ain't never gonna thaw,
It has been frozen for three years now/I have broken vow after vow/To cleanse my brain of all nitroglycerin /But da acid, ain't no everyday aspirin/ It flows freely from my brain to da tip of my toes/Creating unimaginable, anger woes,

Yoyo, over da years you have been an exemplary guide/Loyal, always at my side/But I am now a dyed in wool "Zooiville Thugger" swinger/Acidic nitroglycerin slinger,
Slugging out harbinger after harbinger/With each preacher man mortality zinger/I point my finger/Mock da hypocrisy singer,
A "Karmapucka" dressed in red/That casts shadows over my bed/Whose lies, haunting lyrics/Are da cause of my anger hysterics,
I have no foil /When da nitroglycerin in my veins, begin to boil/Yielding vitriol, explosions/ Sanity implosions,
My dear brutha's death, has me rife with anger/A slave to unclear, and suicidal danger/Insanity's wheels keep on churning/Da nitro in ma veins, keeps on burning,
Brutha "G", buoyed by memories of yo effervescent smiles/ I'm gonna become a marathon running, tooth -ferry/Scamper da 1,942 miles/ To where sits yo cemetery,

Place a daffodil flower basket/ Atop yo casket/Next to it, lay supine/Flutter our "Shared Eyelids", in hopes of having our souls entwine,

Styopos, Yoyo again/In a storm filled with pouring down rain/You some kinda brave/To lay supine, sleep overnight, next to yo brutha's grave, But, please listen, let me be yo guide/I have no intentions to deride/I beg of you, do not use dem nitroglycerin sticks in yo pocket, to blow up this cemetery plot/ Due to yo visions of it becoming, "Reincarnation's Lot".

Though you and your beloved brother/Share "Eyelids of each Other"/Are true birds of a feather/God knows you two will not again be together/Until you die/And someone that truly loves you, kiss your forehead, and place their soul beneath your black bow tie,

Until then/Take on the freedom. fluidity of a wren/Walk on a cloud/Make Yoyo, Brother "G", of you proud,

Acidic nitroglycerin will cease to fuel my aged brain with anger/Will not continue to be an inequalities of death, theory slanger/Yoyo Conshunce will be my guide/Until into mortality's hole, I slide.

DA CLAIRVOYANT

My obsession with sycophants led to my being described as a "Voodoo Clairvoyant", by my donut shop buddies..
Da obsession stems from their notoriety as bootlickers, without any regards for dignity, self-respect, and my take on their lack of character.

In da deep south, from which many underprivileged blacks departed, bootlickers were labeled "house negroes",tis best not to use the correct terms. Anyways, they licked mas'rs feet and were rewarded for keeping him informed, as to what slaves were thinking and doing. They got rewarded handsomely, slept on mas'rs floors, ate well, escaped da fields drudgery, lived a good life.
But, were considered to be enemies of the state by field hands. I put them on the same level with the most despicable mortals in the history of mankind, mass murderers, pedophiles, serial killers, child molesters, assassins, you name it.

My temper boiled over when my boy Joe Sweet,a lifelong sycophant, poked fun at my prediction on the coming of a viral pandemic that would kill millions of innocent people.
He insisted that I had become mentally anemic and was merely a voodoo, fake clairvoyant man, sent directly from the "Land of Noz"... Mention of the "Land of Noz," is a tipping point for any true clairvoyant. Our futuristic powers have given us a peek into that kingdom and we are fully aware of its inhabitants.
I shudder at the thought of being tossed into the same sphere as heathens, atheists, rapists, gossipers, and the like,
Lo and behold, true to my prediction, there comes the mind numbing news that a deadly virus was rapidly spreading across the entire universe. Theories, lies spread rapidly fueled by conspiracy leaks that shook up the world. Cover-ups abounded, then panic set in as world leaders fed the public lie after lie on its origin.
It's Tuesday, donut shop gathering time for retirees, clairvoyants, sycophants, liars, palm readers, ex-jocks, preachers, you name it, we are all there,

This particular Tuesday, mirror no other, because we are all masked men, except my boy Joe Sweet. He is shunned, dared to come within six feet of anyone, or get socked in the mouth. He keeps shouting, "da president of the United States of America sez, we have nothing to worry about. The virus thing is temporary, much like da flu, common cold, other normal maladies."
Someone bellows, "Joe, when is the prez gonna take his jabs.
When was the da last time you licked da prez's' feet?
I see you wearing yo old faded "MADA", Make America Dumb Again, cap, which personifies yo personna.
I heard you just got back from one of them "BOA", Bootlickers of America, rallies in Hicks, Arkansas, held by "SOA", Sycophants of America, inc. Da six o'clock news sez it was a bootlickers paradise with all the president's men in attendance.
Is it true that nobody wore a mask, and that all of you were given a bottle of "Aggafizzity", to abate any, and all, viral symptoms.

Yep, just got back last week, had a blast. Got my bottle of Aggafizzity in my coat pocket'. Why y'all wearing dem masks? All y'all is doing is recycling da air that you breathe.

Morningstein Blackburn, I see you back there gloating, thinking yo prediction has come true. All you Clairvoyants need to stop wid all dem predictions about da future, let's live in da present.
Joe Sweet, my man, we can't have da present without da future. Each tick of da clock goes from present to future. This pandemic thing is for real, we haven't seen anything yet. I closed my eyes the other night, and was frightened by clairvoyant gods dancing in my head. I can still hear them screaming, " run Morningstein, run, towards da west to east rising sun. Here comes da viral pandemic, that is going to inflict immeasurable carnage on da human race, I sez, which way is da west to east rising sun? They exclaimed, "wherever da future is". I think them clairvoyant gods are saying we all are already dead, because da virus is gonna sweep mother earth clean of all its current inhabitants, eventually.
I closed my eyes again and saw no end to this viral explosion which is going to create a whole new galaxy, encumbered by aliens.

There is nowhere to run, nowhere to hide, da virus is visible, invisible, seen, unseen, it is just like da wind, powerful, destructive. I closed my eyes once more, and saw the coming of vaccines, much more effective than your Aggafizzity.
But each dose will mirror the present, be temporary, with da future still up in da air. Every man, woman, child will be affected by da virus in some form or fashion, it is inevitable.
Joe Sweet, you better get yoself a mask, and be da first in line to get jabbed when da vaccine goes public. You are most vulnerable to death due to your underlying health conditions.
If I recall correctly, you have asthma, sugar dibiteus, high blood pressure, epilepsy, emphysema, and worst of all sycophantitis. You cannot lick anymore boots, they carry da virus in its most lethal form.

All of sudden, with da donut shop crowd witnessing it live and in color, Joe Sweet collapses and starts to convulse, with his face turning black as coal. Moe Johnson, in panic mode, yells, "searches his pockets for that bottle of Aggafizzity he was issued at da "MADA" rally. Pour it down his throat and see what happens.
It is s'pose to be a cure all for da virus, according to da president.. Morningstein, Morningstein, what is his future, come the cries of the crowd.

MB, in a hushed tone, declares, he will live to see da future. Call 911 and it's best we all scatter. Do not approach Joe Sweet. If you do so, you will get infected. Forget da bottle of Aggafizzity it is a hoax. Joe Sweet is rushed to a nearby hospital, but has trouble getting admitted, all da beds, ventilators, are taken.

Joe Sweet, strapped to a gurney, regains consciousness screaming, "I can't breathe, I can't breathe. Morningstein, you wuz right, this pandemic thing is for real. You is a high-tiered Clairvoyant, you is not from da "Land of Noz", you is true as da "Wizard of Oz."

If I gits a venturlater, and survive, I is gonna stop licking boots, feets, no mas "MADA", rallies, "SOA" conventions. All I want to do is get back to da donut shop on Tuesday and chew da fat.

Joe Sweet passed away quietly, two days before reaching age seventy. He did not get a chance to cross da "Three Sco-n-Ten", time line, to see what lies beyond da present.

"IN CAHOOTS"

My name is Augusus Lee Blackburn. People call me Gussie for short, because they have difficulty pronouncing Augusus. Many claim my name is missing the letter "T" and that it should be inserted.
I counter by informing that my Grandma Emily placed the name upon me, and what grandmas want, grandmas get,

Being the son of a sharecropper, brought with it many slave driven experiences that cling to the soul forever and a day. Chopping cotton,, shucking corn, plowing fields, digging potatoes, were everyday routines, along with whatever else came with life on a plantation.
The enemies of the land were da 'house Skiggas", down in da dirt, bootlickers, brown- nosers, mealy mouthed, rats, of da boss.
The one term that looped all of them together, so happens to be "sycophant". They were spies, licked masr's boots and were always "in Cahoots" trying to find ways to get outta da fields into da "Big House".. Sycophants would turn on their own mamas if it meant the difference between the fields and masr's quarters.
For a long time, during my early years, I had no idea what the term "in Cahoots" meant, and its relationship to the word sycophant. I thought it was the name of slave quarters up the river or something.
"In Cahoots" was a familiar cry amongst slave driven field hands, while toiling under the red hot sun, in cotton fields, back home

Then one day, when I was around ten or eleven years old, my Uncle Joe and the foreman came and snatched Billy Bob Jones from out of the fields and tied him to a China Ball tree, and summoned all people on the plantation to come witness the brutal spectacle.
They beat him unmercifully with a sap laden leather strap that left scars nearly matching the length of the strap, itself.
They brutalized Billy Bob in broad daylight, in front of men, women, and children. I was frightened to death.
All around da slave quarters, there was the cry, "Cousin Julie is in "In Cahoots"., she licked mas'rs boots". Billy Bob became the shell of a man and later died, with little fanfare.

Word got around that my dear cousin julie Mae Spurlock, exposed Billy Bob's plan of insurrection, The plan was simple, no danger to field hands, The plan was to march kids up to the "Big House" Halloween night for trick or treats.
All natives found out, later on, that suchuch was forbidden on da plantation, because Mas'r wife was afraid of ghosts.
Cousin Julie sneaked up to the big house and got word to Masr' on the plan and was therefore "in Cahoots."
She was rewarded with a job as a maid in da Big House, and was rarely seen or heard from again by folks on da plantation. In church, her name was not to be spoken by anyone.
She was a "Sycophant" and any mention of her was a sin..

All the old folks on da plantation knew that cousin Julie hated Billy Bob because he sired a son for Annie B, who was later on found out to cousin Julie's half sister,
Cousin Julie and Billy Bob,, were just two weeks from getting hitched, when the news broke. She was furious, and threw the engagement ring into Cane River.
She got her revenge by being "In Cahoots", watched solemnly as Billy Bob, suffered through the beating wearing the boots she had bought for their wedding day.
She was a "Sycophant, a brown noser, a bootlicker, servile, rat. It was rumored that cousin Julie, later on, became the Masr's mistress, and had six little ones for him.

It is Halloween night, and flashbacks of my days on da piantation, bring to the forefront da haunting screams of, "Cousin Julie is "In Cahoots",, she licked Masr's boots".
Images of Billy Bob screaming, moaning, still sends chills up and down my spine.
As the world turns, "In Cahoots" aptly describes the current state of affairs, as bootlickers, brown nosers,mealy mouthed, rats, climb ladders of success much more rapidly than we field hands.
Nowadays "In Cahoots", licking boots, brown nosing, fawning, are true means and ways of getting to the "Big House, '

I often wonder what impact Billy Bob's insurrection plan would have had on all of us. if he had not been "in Cahooted", our lives could have been "Re- booted.. '
Might have made a difference in Masr's mindset, and reversed roles of field hands, and house Skiggas.

I stand at my door with a basket of Halloween goodies, and smile when a youngster in a Spiderman mask yells " we want some candies shaped like cowboy boots,or we are gonna be "in Cahoots, with da goblin who loots". I smile as I close the door thinking, very little has changed over the years. I guess we will always be "in Cahoots", with something, in one way or another.

"DA DAYS OF MY LIFE"

Which is more prevalent in "Da Days of Life", feelings of being Nobody's, No-body, or relations of being Somebody's, Some-body?. Let's define each, according to Merriam Webster, to get a better perspective.
Nobody- A noun,, no person, not anyone. One of no significance, influence.
No- body- A pronoun,, no person, not anybody.
Somebody- A noun, a person of position, importance. Some-body- A pronoun, one or some person of unspecified, or indefinite identity.

Well, I can't speak for anyone else, without question, "Nobody", best describes my state of being. I am now an octogenarian, stuck in a time tunnel, with no more pages to turn.
I've inhabited mother earth for over eight decades, and few people even know my name, let alone of any significant contribution I've made to the advancement of mankind. As days fly off into the mist, faster than a weaver's shuttle, I find myself trying to hold back the hands of time, to no avail. To make things worse, battles with Covid -19, breed abject feelings of despair,

Nearing the end of life, I find myself clinging to remembrances of earlier years when there was a tinge of feeling as though I was "Somebody" .
As a high strung interscholastic basketball coach, adoration from players, fans, instilled a sense of belonging to something larger than self. Those were the good ol days, when passage of time was an afterthought. I was "Da Days of Life", in perpetual motion, from sunrise to sunset.
Flux of time was never met with resistance, there were no timekeepers, just fire lit dreams of winning a city championship. We as a people strive to be at peace with ourselves, but keep getting knocked off our feet by life's never ending travails. The old axiom, "if it ain't one thing, it's another", has become a ruling truth of consequence. If it's not caustic fears of the SARs pandemic, then we have mass shootings, even in places of worship,

The vigor of looking forward to the next day has been replaced with,, I wish tomorrow never comes". Veracity with which falsehoods now strangle the norm, turn "Da Days of Life", into unmitigated strife.

Da Days of Life, religion tires now roll on bumpy grounds, as proponents of atheism and devotees of christianity crash in the heat of da night, without a murmur from either party.
Mega churches have supplanted da neighborhood homes to worship, for the most part, as flamboyant throwers of the words of God, flood television screens.
Social media has no boundaries, and kids as young as three, keep heads buried in cellular phones, mesmerized by fantasies of epic proportions.
Lines that once separated truth from consequence have been obliterated by moral decay of society.. Da Days of Life are now being ambushed by monsters, who have total disregard for rules of law, designed to protect democracy..
Violence, hatred of "Some- bodies", have created bushels of "No-bodies.

Plethora of aging senior citizens are of the opinion that those around us are simply waiting for mortality to collect its dues from "No- bodies.",routinely tossed into unmarked graves.
"Da Days of My Life", are no more, or less, than that of ninety nine percent of the population..But, I have found ways to be at peace with my current state of being.
One day at a time, easier said than done, at least puts things in proper perspective. As an octogenarian, I have accepted the consequence of time and have become thankful for every minute of the hour. that comes my way. Father Time is undefeated and will continue to be, long after I have departed. Nobody, No-body, Somebody, Some-body, they have been given the reins to circumscribe "Da Days of My Life".

"HARD TIMES"

I no longer have "soles", beneath my feet, I am soulless.

Damn, I'm down to eating donut holes for breakfast.

Gotta exercise, ten push-ups, severe heartburn.

Depressed, I run to avoid running.

Weakened, my exercise routine now consists of rolling over out of bed.

My life mirrors Humpty Dumpty, I had a great fall...

A hobo asked to borrow my cap.

Got caught stealing a pack of chewing gum, sentence.., forty years of hard labor,

Hard times, not difficult finding misery.. rhymes.

Holy mackerel, diesel fuel, $9.99 cents per gallon... where is my walking cane?

No need to wonder why all pet food shelves are empty... human consumption.

I need a stimulus check, worse than a woodpecker needs to peck.

Truthfully, yesterday I was so hungry, I imbibed skin from one of my golf balls.

Never, ever, thought I would get down to the point whereby finger nail clippings became a delicacy.

Hard times lead to unmerciful crimes

Broke, poverty stroke, birds of a feather, in sunshine or stormy weather.

Hard times, the 99 cents store was shuttered due to lack of 99 cents items.

Cm'on, prices are getting a bit out of hand, asking sixteen dollars for a Big Mac combo,

Infectious Inflation, Defectious Discombobulation,,, during hard times, one in da same,

Da Prez, ferrying trillions overseas, while we Americans subsist on dog fleas.

Hard times… bad climes, agree? Pandemic…masks, recycled air,,, busted eardrums.

Isn't it a downright dirty shame,, we humans can no longer share the air we breathe.

Hard times, brutal, lethal…mass killings, homelessness.

Hard times lead to cannibalism, we kill, feed off each other.

Hard times… when tomorrow is worse than today.

Hard times. . . more self-appointed, storefront preachers, than educated, school teachers.

SLAVERY BRIDGES

To aptly describe "Slavery Bridges" in relation to negroes, during the thirties, forties, fifties, one would have to be a victim of such obnoxious mistreatment of the underclass, to grasp its magnitude..
There is no way it can be sugar coated, no matter the attempts by historians to bury the past.
School buildings alone, put one behind the eight ball. Many were makeshift structures from old houses, churches, barns.
For eight years my learning pool was a converted, country home, which sat smack dab in the middle of a cow pasture, bounded by a small canal on one side, a huge cornfield in front, bisected by a gravel road.
My memory pane is frosted, but a major "Slavery Bridge", thwarting equality, was lack of healthcare for the disinherited. Charity hospitals staffed with ill trained physicians, were commonplace and led to lifetime miseries with one swipe of a scalpel. When recalling life experiences, during my formative years, quackery takes center stage because I was a picture of bad health, and fell into the care of many mal-practitioners.
Unfortunately at medical institutions in the deep south, malpractice was as common as falling leaves in autumn.
Schools, higher learning institutions were built to racially separate, rather than educate. Separate and unequal, was the unwritten law of the land, void of any sequel.
I will attempt to defrost my memory pane with a sketchy "rime and reason" of the seasons of my life, as I struggled to cross "Slavery Bridges".

Unforgettable, Bethel School/ A lil white shack/Both, my drowning, learning, pool/ Was taught to be nobody's fool/ How to keep humpty dumpty off my back,
My mama stressed,never wallow in poverty's lair/Climb the education ladder, stair by stair/Call a spade a spade/Always try to be leader of da higher learning parade,

In my frosted memory pane/I can still envision our school bus contraption/ On bald,slick tires, trying to hold traction/As it roared down Kaffay Lane/I

shudder at images of how the "bus" would lean, slide/While rounding the steep, Papa Bend curve/My heart would stop beating with every swerve/I thought the devil was along for the ride,
Hand me down books, desks, chairs, were in full play/In the path of learning, many obstacles stood in the way/But, for many, education was the only hope/ To avoid poverty's hangman's rope,
The abc's of life/Were fraught with toils and strife/Many throats were slit by racial hatred, ever sharpening knife/No matter/Perseverance was our spiritual batter.

Commodity sourced meals were free/But full, healthy meals, not to be /One image in my mind, forever lies/That of a slice of Ms.Mae Lisa's peach pies,
Memories of gathering wood to fire up the old stove/Add embers to my nostalgia trove/We had a basketball court, littered with grass/Made it difficult to bounce pass/But, boy oh boy/ It brought to many of us, immeasurable joy,'
The hands of time, move on and tis no use crying over spilled milk, as grandma loved to say. During formative years, as a sharecropper's son, lessons on inequities in life were plowed into my soul and irrigated by spiritual waters, sublime,
Second class citizenship was the law of the land for black folks, written with pens dripping with blood of slaves.
No amount of reparations can pay for evils of slavery, and wounds that never heal.
Country folks back then were very resilient, tossed many obstacles aside, and found their places in the sun.., despite being shackled by chains of disenfranchisement.
Reflections from "Slavery Bridges", are void of ridges, splatter all over the place, bringing into play lurid waters of circumspection.
Da tastes of slavery, poverty bites,, remain bitter as gall.
Got my flamethrower in hand, tis time for all "Slavery Bridges" to go up in flames, no mo poverty, racial,enslavement games.

DA GAP

"Da Gap", is the brainchild of one Styopos J. Buck, who now finds himself running from da hounds of father time.
Da "Septo-Octo", a ten year period between ages seventy and eighty, closes rapidly, while da body is being ravaged by mortality's wolves.

Years, in "Da Gap",shed rapidly like autumn leaves, as. winds of Circumstance, Clairvoyance, Lady Luck, Destiny, Fate, blow like hurricane gales.
Aged ones are dumped into conundrums, littered with ghosts, fears of the past, present, future,
The world, as a whole, is changing at a dizzying speed, and "Gappers" are finding it difficult to keep pace. Trying to adapt to new technology, social trends, leaves many blowing in the wind.

Amazing,one can sit on a stool in Omaha, and converse with a relative in Nova Scotia, by striking a few numbers on a cellular phone. Mind you, with that feed, comes "Facetime" whereby you can view gray hairs on grandpa's head, that he refuses to shave.

To those of us who find ourselves in "Da Gap", the past no longer mirrors the present, because many events of today are beyond the pale and stretch imagination to its outer limits.

Social media outlets control the airwaves, and hold us prisoners to their every truth, lie, and consequence, `, A very thin line divides mantras of the good, bad, ugly, as truths, lies, bury themselves under the same mosaic quilts, diffusing all tenets of distinction.

Missteps in a "Gapper' ' own neighborhood, can lead to assaults, ramifications, beyond the pale.
With SARS as its enforcer, an elderly gent can get maimed, for sneezing at the wrong time.
"Gappers" have been thrust into a viral pandemic quagmire that has turned kin against kin, brother against brother, with teachings of the church being tossed to da wind.

Tis no more 'take the road less traveled, gospel", because da road no longer exists. All roads of true happiness have been trampled upon, wiping out division lines, leading to head on collisions with reality.

Styopos loves to bellow, "No matter how fast da "Gap" closes, I got my metaphors, allegories, similes", to keep my imagination warm, I ain't ready for mortality's farm".

Quite a statement coming from an aged fella, who recoils at any mention of da "Will of God",
"We are on our own . Each duck, its own waddle. God does not intervene in everyday existence, survival", a belief fervently espoused..

Styopos became one angry man, upon the untimely death of his beloved brother, as a myocardial infarction, deprived him of any travel in "Da Gap". The devastating event left him stranded, alone, in a wilderness of despair, chased by wolves of despair.

Fast moving rows in "Da Gap", can be ones of acidic bitterness, regrets, as da time clock never resets, and begets misery.

Lifelong handicaps are doozies, and worsen as "Da Gap", readies to snap shut. Having to adlib in life, minus a self esteem bib, to deflect physical, mental, shortcomings, is a suffocating handicap that tightens as years bury themselves in fields of grass.

A chance union of sperm with egg, can yield gruesome consequences, plethora of birth defects, that are rarely reverted, leading to life spans of unmerciful, suffering,

It is said that one can actually hear the creaking gate of " Da Gap", as it readies to close. Tis declared to be a frightening experience, that further warps a dementing mind,

"Do not expect a bed of roses/When "Da Gap" closes/Time is no longer on your side/You have entered da land where pale ghosts ride/Father Time, is now your shadow/Wherever you travel, it will follow,

It is said that once one turns "Eight-O'/Ill winds start to blo/Age denial/ Goes up on trial/Nowhere to run/There comes a west to east, setting sun".

Da Septo-Octo Gap / Ten year human maze trap/Da brain begins to unsnap/Mortality wings, flap, flap

Age 77, in three years, "Da Gap", closes/You better smell yourself some roses/Bucket list/Fling it into the mist.

"SILENCE OF THE AM"

Silence of the Am/Mutes sound/Freezes ds soul's bedlam/Each echo rebound/Quietens anger demons when I'm alone/That seek to devour me bone by bone,
Silence of the Am/Frees da mind of any sound log jam/Combatant of nature's fields of sound/Tis my soul's stillness impound/As i seek seek to ratchet my soul up to another level of contentment/Free of evil intent.
Silence of the AM/Sublime/Mutes tick tocks of father time/Rivals the quietude in horns of a ram,
I am often rattled, embattled, by what is perceive to be inequality in deaths of the good, while da bad lives on,
Demons of doubt, raise their ugly heads, and throw the inner workings of the "Am", into turmoil, as it wallows in climes of mistrust as to whom or what, controls mortality's levers.
One can become bewildered as good, well intentioned disciples of Christ, are randomly robbed of time on earth, while vagabonds, heathens, thieves, liars, atheists, live on.
Silence of the Am/Goes up on trial/Da devil takes control of faith in the Almighty's noise dial/No more quietness in horns of da ram,
Silence of the Am/Much needed, when over a cuckoo's nest

I'm blown/Silence shattered by sounds from the unknown/Life becomes a sham,
Silence of the Am/My hallowed dam/Holds back noises of discontent/ Allow me to repent/Clear doubts in da Almighty, log jam,
With my brother's death, communication with a few species of nature's winged animals that flourish on flowers in my backyard, has been a blessing in disguise.
Sounds from fluttering wings of monarch butterflies have raised my level of hearing to rare heights..
I enter my mute chamber, in the southeast corner of the yard, shut my brain down, except to sounds of nature, and traverse fields of, " Silence of the Am"
"Silence of the Am"/ Muteness within/Be it human, ram/Tis da soul's kingpin/During times of discord/Tempers doubt, loss of faith in da Lord, .

A contented silence state of being," frees the human mind of log jams, when sanity, insanity spar, and the brain rattles ajar,

When such events occur, "Silence of the Am" must divert internal spears that can shatter one's spiritual glass, and lead to mental discombobulation,,

I am a firm believer in" Silence of the Am", but also realize that it is meaningless, if it does not fertilize a barren soul,

I swing on the vine which supports the notion that"Silence of the Am", is most productive when imagination is at its highest peak. A time in which the mind flies open and swallows up all sounds of discontent,

"HEAVEN/HELL/Purgatory", landing spots of the human soul upon expiration, are they of muted silence , or unknown sounds. I rather not guess, "Silence of the Am"/Pure/Impure/Be your own horns of the ram,

"Silence of the Am', has a backdraft that is serene, and its muteness quietens resounding echoes from insanity's whistles,
Demons within one's soul feed upon weakness in spirit, and can become apocalyptic in nature .
I staunchly support tenets of "Silence, no matter the sphere of origin, because in so many instances it is more mystic, serene than sound. .
True "Silence of the Am", awaits us all, but don't be afraid of that which one cannot control. Souls are muted, but spirits live on,

Recently while resting on the shores of "Silence of the Am', during a strange dream, I met my"Silence of the Am', shade, Prophet Sam., tagging along on a climb to Purgatory. The trek took me along ascending mountain ledges, landscapes, mirroring the path followed on my journey to procure my mythical "Five Leaf Clover".
There were sounds, sprinkled with muted periods of silence, making it difficult to distinguish one entity from the other.
I was quick to ask Prophet Sam, "sound, silence,, can we have one without the other?
"Impossible, was the reply, because they are one half of each other, both yielded from enlivened appendages of the brain,

Silence favors darkness, the other light., interchangeable at times, you hear what you hear, see what you see, mutely, acutely.
Once a person maximizes "Silence of the Am" to the highest degree, it permeates nuggets of protection against unwanted sounds".
Before I could open my mouth, Prophet Sam was usurped by darkness, sending me into a freefall off a cliff as the dream ended,
I sit on a stone in my backyard, reflecting on the aborted dream, communicating in silence with three monarch butterflies that form a circular homing squad, along with occasional sightings of bees, mosquitoes, gnats, birds.. Prophet Sam, though only in a dream, left an imprint on my brain "Silence of the Am", comes into full play as I query as to whether or not these winged animals, that buzz around me, can detect sound. They create sound via their homings, but can they distinguish sound from silence.

To save what is left of my sanity, I abandon all thoughts of the climb that occurred in the dream with Prophet Sam, flip pages in the Book of Sty, and refresh myself with the empowering lines that have become stabilizers during times of extreme periods of "Silence of the Am", . " They read, "Death has neither time nor season, no time, nor reason, all mortals are subject to the same, expiration flame".. The lines are bluntly stated, but ring true, "Sounds of the Am", can be breeding grounds for doubt, loss of faith in the Almighty by christian disciples whose beliefs have been weakened by perceived inequities in deaths,

"Silence of the Am" /"Sounds of the Am", are interwoven, .ESD/ESP, needles that weave imagination threads, in the human mind. Death has no checkmates, and is exclusive of time parameters, with one mirroring the other, Tis sad, but true,

I love silence/Rids the soul of pestilence/Creates resilience/Readily clears one conscience,

"Silence of the Am/Formidable as horns of a ram/Key to joy , happiness/ Tis its own witness/ To each, its own/Spiritually, flown.

Ashes to ashes. dust to dust, says it all when it comes to the significance of an individual. Perishings of human beings, ain't no different than that of ants, reptiles, elephants, butterflies, sharks. All carcasses decompose to replenish the earth's crust.

The hour of my brother's death is sadder each passing day.
I can hear the rush of sound and fury ringing in my ears, pitch forking, my "Silence of the Am". into sounds of fury. Testily, I become bereft with anger, and try to refill my soul with thoughts of the good times we experienced. Goodness, righteousness, hypocrisy, no matter, same fish in a barrel, as far as death is concerned. We all exist in the realm of its circular firing squad.

I will always keep "Silence of the Am", in my hip pocket, to stifle ever increasing sounds, whims, of mortality's roosters.
I owe my departed brother more than frothings from anger seeds, during imaginary bouts with Satan, da Almighty, and ghosts of Saint Christopher. Being over half way through the "Septo –Octo Gap leaves me vulnerable to various flanges of mortality, so each ounce of silence, a treasure.
My sad hour is fast approaching, turning my attention away from ashes to ashes, dust to dust, towards grasses of immortality, to enrich fast dwindling days left on mother earth,
Tis time to weave my legacy quilt, forsaking all tenets of slothfulness and worry. Eat, drink and be merry, is gonna be my rallying cry during my cabaret. Extreme joy is my goal, which will lead to untangling of nooses from around my neck and shedding shards of unmitigated anger that have sucked the life out of me.
"Silence of the Am", will juxtapose, from time to time, as "Sounds of the Ram", with the latter being a runner of my brother's spirit,
I have tarried too long in shadows of doubt, tis time to hitch up my britches and get on with living, as if there is no tomorrow.
I will die alone, so why fool myself by thinking that others really care when my time is up.
I shall become a vagabond with a cream of da crop mantra, shed all life's failure corn shucks, toss them to the wind, and never look back . No one will ever again disturb the peace of "Silence of the Am", which shall be of extreme benevolence.
Rudiments of faith will relieve my soul of all constraints of irrelevance, as I toot my Metal Pea whistle, to silence all demons within.

Plucking my silence strings, until the caged bird sings, will lead to total recall of the days I was proud as a peacock, chasing high school basketball championships,
Cabaret has good times, which are gonna be my "Silence of the Am". Goodbye needles of discontent, welcome, "Squalms" of purposeful intent,

There are no more shadows of doubt, on my bedroom loft., such have been replaced by cascading images of beautiful angels, flapping wings in rhythmic fashion,
Isn't imagination a beautiful gift, that grows its own orchard of roses. I say to myself, sleep well Styopos,J. Buck, sleep well, long gone is the ringing of mortality bells in your ears, no mo sum of all fears.,
"Silence of the Am", gravitational pull, empowers me to pirouette on clouds of joy, back flipping against the backdrop of a west to east setting sun.

Leaves of Nirvana

"AWAKENING"

Like being struck by bolts of lightning /Amidst pouring rain/Over and over again/My soul is set afire by the coming of a spiritual Awakening".
Gone are drastic feelings of being akin to desert tumbleweeds blowing in da wind, leading me to shout glory hallelujah.
Spiritual awakenings are spawned from miracles in the spirit, and spring eternal hope in those wishing to enter life's citadel of happiness..

Prior to my most recent " Awakening', mortality's circular firing squad had bullets aimed at my head that I was not aware of. Accepting the realities of old age opened my eyes, and awakened me to the hum of cartridges and its bullets flying everywhere.
No mortal is immune to fears of what the afterlife may bring, but spiritual awakenings ease feelings of discontent.
Our visions of Heaven, and its flowering fields of countenance, become faith stones that allay fears of dying.
We cannot sit with legs crossed, laughing, joking, while Father Time breathes down our necks.
Instead, we must accept reality and prepare for the inevitable. There is nothing wrong with keeping alive dreams of immortality, but we must prepare for that one second divide, between living/non-living,

Awakenings are ecclesiastic, yield frost bites from the past, present, future, and at times, squeeze bushels of joy out of morsels of sadness. Subliminal "Awakenings" spewed from deep crevices of the subconscious mind, belong solely to the dreamer.
Dreams, awakenings, readily flush the past into the present, and can be scintillating in nature.
There is a thin line between sanity, insanity, when we are being swept back and forth by winds of discontent..
Nocturnal dreams, imagination,awakenings, walk hand in hand, and have led to discoveries, inventions that have changed the world for the betterment of mankind
Much to our dismay, awakenings can also be storefronts of extreme sadness,

How many times have you had dreams, awakenings, centered around the departed,, too many to name...

There are also those that seem like deja vu, all over again. Recalls from class, family, reunions, can either uplift or drop one into the claws of "Beasts of failure".

There is no denying that awakenings travers fields of the good, bad and ugly, leaving weeds of hopelessness. or flowers of happiness..

Spiritual awakenings are spark plugs that ignite embers in the soul that fuels imagination, which is the lifeblood of mankind's innovative nature. Ashes from the past flow from generation to generation, leaving legacy trails as proof of one having passed this way. An individual, no matter how we look at it, is much like a particle of dust, destined for mortality's bottomless cauldron.

Life yields slings, arrows of misfortune, which oftentimes batter mortals to a pulp,

MY DEAR BROTHER, was in da glorified period of his life span, ready to reap fruition from being a dedicated Christian soldier, when a massive heart attack struck him down.

In a fraction of a second divide, he became a seed upon the wind, swept into oblivion, leaving me as a pod with no pea.

My anger refuses to subside, surrealistic dreams have kept us in touch, providing relief from abject misery.

I have been able to keep alive dreams of the heart via precious memories,, and all other spiritual straws available, courtesy of an "Awakening".

In cold blood came my "Awakening" to the fact that death is final,culminating in ashes to ashes, dust to dust,at times, tossed to the wind.

The struggle is mighty when it comes to understanding why the good die young,, while the bad lives on. Courtesy of a sudden, massive "myocardial Infarction", my dear brother disappeared from the face of mother earth, and I find it impossible to accept.

His sudden departure opened my eyes to the vulnerability of us all, when it comes to the final reckoning,

Human mortality stretches far beyond the pale of reasoning and has no borders. To christen the plurality of my much needed spiritual "Awakening". I run towards the west to east setting sun, no longer in need of dodging bullets from mortality's circular firing squad.

Moonlight, sunlight, must continue to brighten the path of my footsteps, as I creep closer to da "Great Divide's" final reckoning.

Awakenings collided, during a lascivious virus pandemic,as da good, da bad, da ugly, were swept into unmarked graves, amidst hypocrite strewn wailings of, "Tis God's will".
My "Awakening" has empowered me to shoot holes in such lunacy, because the Almighty is far removed from day to day activities of mankind, and is deaf to human wailing.
Climate change, laboratory viruses, define the saying, "we reap what we sow"
My Awakening, a shining, silver lining, picture show in panavision, , has opened mine eyes to life's rules of order.
We become feckless elfs, if we rely on "Da Lord" to rescue us from earthly evils. The Lord does not dip its mighty hands into earthly conditions we create, on our own free will and accord.
Climate change is "God's will", sheer nonsense to the highest degree. Prior to my "Awakening", I clamored to blame "That", which is blameless, for lack of spirit and conviction.
I was a tumbleweed being blown back and forth between sanity, insanity. Da wind bloweth, where mankind not knoweth, as he reaps what he soweth". Many scrolls of life are written in unknown tones, undecipherable to mankind, which lead to wrath filled orders of day to day living.
Da devil mocks, as we bludgeon precious time on earth, seeking to define that which is far beyond the reaches of mankind. Even Lucifer knows not, from where comes da sun, moon, stars.
We mortals, oftentimes, wallow in apathy, seeking sympathy from our own souls, void of impunity.
The art of living becomes even more disordered, as paws of Father Time tighten around our throats. The ruthlessness of daily routines takes its toll and we start back pedaling, seeking cover underneath quilts of christianity, totally immune to the undeniable truth that Father Time is undefeated.
As life's game clock winds down, we find ourselves out of timeouts, panic sets in, but there is nowhere to run nor hide.. We drink fills of survival juices, but yet become prisoners within our own souls.
"There is always hope/We just have to cling to our spiritual rope/Never mope/Accept our sure to come slides down mortality's slope".

My "Awakening" shook free my longed stilled "Lute of da heart", with its resounding strings of spiritual benevolence.

Reverberations of my now active "Lute", ignite embers in my soul that burn like wildfires in Autumn.. There is music in the air that most surely emanates from heaven's shore.

I shout hallelujah, hallelujah, while turning back flips in tune with a west to east setting sun. I just have to compose that which is yet to be sung, to give my "Lute" the christening it so richly deserves. My life's Emmy award winning music is yet to come.

Continually, vibrations from heart's once stilled lute, resonate throughout my soul. The vibrations are rampant, and have a calming effect, which is serene. Faith in the homings of the soul, have refreshed my will to live beyond, ever present, thresholds of pain. My knees throb, cannot I swing my seven iron freely, but my nerves are steely, as I toss spitballs at mortality's mob..

The west to east sun has taken on a mystic shade, allowing use of its corona rays to strengthen my weakened eyes.

I now take comfort in knowing full well that rays that sprung forth my "Awakening" stretch from the backside of the sun, to the deepest depths of oceans, engulfing all in between, seen, unseen..

I hope to spend my final days, in good health, with earned wealth, enabling me to pick flowers of success, happiness, from fields of endearment.

I will wave my "Five Leaf Cover Scrolls, in honor of my "Awakening", in defiance of all false prophecies.. The scrolls, Circumstance, Clairvoyance, Coincidence,Lady Luck), Destiny, Fate, define my beliefs. on the sojourn from cradle to tomb.

I favor all laws that relieve "Da Almighty" of tenets of heresy, false prophecy, and hypocrisy, such as the crowning of "God's Will".

The following sayings define my "Awakenings", and serve as gospel for day to day survival.

1. Soul on ice/Roll the dice/Set sail/Made, I have no fear of death, a holy grail.
2. Believe, beauty within a star/ Can be seen from afar/ Tis much deeper than its light/Heavenly bright. .
3. My "Awakening", far superior to my seven iron golf swing.

4. Throughout this horrific virus pandemic, my "Awakening" has been my wicker, its candle light continues to flicker.
5. Da sun never ceases to shine, orders day, night, to entwine, that da Almighty, sanctified, have I lied.
6. My "Awakening", refills its own spiritual ink well.
7. Beyond the pale, hypocrites exhale, die of thirst, no matter who's first.
8. False prophecy, no leniency, rules of life, laid, enough said.

ME-D-DA LORD

Lord I'm back again/We need to talk,Mind if we take a walk/Though its drizzling rain, I have some pressing needs/My heart bleeds,

I feel lost, alone/My soul has turned to stone/Lost faith in the preacher man /Too often riles da sermon, "Tis God's Plan"/"/Monologues on how a "backslider" can be forgiven seventy-seven times/Even for sins of the flesh crimes,
The "backslider" gave the church a new front door/A new parquet floor, Do monies dropped in the tithes bin/Redeem sins,

Further Lord, why is there such a discrepancy/In terms of Your role in life expectancy/ My golfing buddy was dedicated, every Sunday "front slider"/ But bang, he was felled unexpectedly by a mortality spider,

Last Sunday the "backslider" rolled into church drunk/As a skunk/Dropped five hundred dollars in the tithes bin/The preacher man kept saying, "da Lord redeems each and every sin",

Now Lord, why did "You" let my buddy die?/ Watch as he was dumped into mortality weeds/While the "backslider" thrived on "redemption seeds/ My buddy got nary a slice of survival pie,
Lord, I am totally confused by this life/death thing/ Am I a sitting duck/ At the mercy of impulsive Lady Luck/A puppet on a string,
Styopos, "I" am the universe's only "Single," /"I" do not intermingle/ With lives of mortals temper/Nor damper,

"I" favor no form of life as its "Keeper"/Once born, each living form becomes its own sower, reaper/Back slider, middle slider, front slider/ Their scents are the same to life's mortality spider,

The preacher man has every right to do his thing/He is subject to the same end of life sting/Unequivocally, no amount of money put in the tithes bin/Redeems one solitary sin,

Without impunity/Immunity/Not ever again shall you infer that "I" let your beloved buddy die/"I" grant each mortal only one blasphemy lie, "I" listen, then become a"Onesider"/ Showering venom a million times more powerful than that of a mortality spider.
Stay true to your beliefs in validity of the "Five Leaf Clover Scrolls/ "I" have sanctified them as having clarity, purity of thunder rolls/ Circumstance,Clairvoyance, Lady Luck, Destiny, Fate/To them, in them, all life forms supplicate,
Styopos, it is way past time for you to cleanse your soul of anger seeds/Or your mind will begin to scatter like tumbleweeds/ Wafting you back and forth between sanity, insanity/Alzymus Tunnel is the resting place for such calamity,

Lord,I wholeheartedly agree/It is very slippery on the downhill side of the mortality slope/ Where I now happen to be/Time, life, death, have begun to interlope/My buddy's death has me scapegoating/In the next breath, sugarcoating/Life's trials , tribulations/No revelations,
Styopos, "I" am mankind's creator/Not a fire, brimstone perpetrator/The preacher man is an orator/Not a right, wrong, arbitrator,
Can you truthfully say that your buddy "E" was a victim of circumstance/ Lacked a sense of clairvoyance/And that no other scroll came into play/ Before Father Time commenced to check, slay,
"I" am really impressed with your clarity in expressing nature's laws of existence/With persistence/Tagging those that actually control human events/Sinful repents,
There comes a time when science is overwhelmed by common sense / Truth has its own universal firewall of defense/Order/Border,,
A very thin line separates, at times, what is false from what is true/The same might be said of back slider and front slider personna/ To each its own karma/ But, in the end, the truth always collects its due,

So refrain from judging motives of the "preacher man"/Don't get worked up over the truth or consequence of the tithes pan/Your place of worship needs contributors/ As well as donators,

Every man has the right to decide/ To either back slide or front slide/Do not become a tithes pan inhibitor/Many blessings are stored upon plates of a contributor,

Styopos, at your ripe old age/You probably know, it won't be long before you exit life's stage/Soon the curtain will fold/ Tis time to be bold,
Will you leave your fellowman so much as a legacy brick, shingle?/ Or simply memories of your ashes to ashes, dust to dust sprinkle/As you become a wind driven dust particle/ Your mundane life span captured in a seventeen word back page obituary article,

At the funeral ,tears flowed when with trembling lips you gave your farewells/Fought back tear swells/Got the feeling of being alone/Your heart turned to stone,
Within that séance,it was if you got struck by a lightning bolt/Soul in revolt/Laced with thoughts of wasted years/You fighting to hold back tears
The realization that your soul brother was gone forever, plummeted you into depths of despair/Unable to accept the truth that life is not fair/Nor even/Steven,,

Yes Lord,At my buddy's funeral/ Stonily, I sat on a pew/Amongst friends, chosen few/With feelings of it being surreal/Staring at his casket/ Atop which sat a red rose flower basket.

Lord, such was an anger filled moment of exasperation/Got knocked off my feet by winds of trepidation/ Soul paralyzed by the brutality, finality of death/ It was as though I was subsisting on my last breath,

Styopos,in parting, "I" leave you with these truths of advice/Do not ever think that death favors men or mice/Every living entity will get burnt by the ashes to ashes,dust to dust flame/As entities of the balance the population game,

Thank you Lord for explaining the art of living in ways I comprehend/ Thoughts on life, death,I now amend/ Can now see clearly now our meeting the role of the preacher man/ I will refrain from questioning merits of the tithes pan,

I also fully accept the truth that life expectancy/And its insolvency/Are interwoven, inextricable natural events/And I seek forgiveness for my loss of faith dissents,

Styopos, "I" favor your beliefs in powers of our meeting as apparitions/ Stratified by perdition's/ Infinite tenets of imagination/Hallucination , "I" admonish you to treasure your beliefs and steer them free of all superstitions, doubts, on the coming and going of an individual.
Thank you again Lord, for the common sense talk /During our existential walk/In which I garnered a few nuggets of respect for the "preacher man"/ Will donate my fair share to the tithes pan,

Lord, I am slowly gaining power over the anger bracelet around my neck / That at times pushes me towards being an insanity wreck/Tis an albatross/ When memories, images,sounds, recollections of my soul brother, crisscross, Styopos, during periods of extreme anger/One becomes a lone ranger/A discombobulated mess/In a sin filled wilderness,
Lord, next time I ask that we meet underneath my favorite eucalyptus tree/Down by the river side/Where my departed ones, pale ghosts ride/ Maybe by that time I'll be anger free.

DIS OL SOUL OF MINE

Dis ol soul of mine, gonna be anger free, anger free, anger free, as I sit with legs crossed beneath da china ball tree,
I'm gonna let it twang, let it twang, let it twang, as I become a member of da "5 leaf Clover Gang,

Dis ol soul of mine, I'm gonna let it shine, let it shine, let it shine, as i walk da line, with a "5 Leaf Clover in hand/To join da Lord's heaven on earth, band.
Lord, Dis ol soul of mine, let it hum, let it hum, let it hum with melodies of mother on da piano, daddy on a harmonica, Elsie Mae on a saxophone, brother Glenn on a drum.

SCRIPTURES/SQUALMS/SASA

Lord have mercy on my son,for he is an epileptic and suffers severely; for he often falls into the fire and often into the water."/ Matthew 1:15

"As for man his days are as grass, as a flower of the field, so he flourisheth, for the wind passeth over it and it is gone, and the place thereof shall know it no more." Psalm 103:15-16

Lord, I am worn, better days now those of wind swept dust, creeping closer to becoming fauna of the earth's crust But, with You as my guiding light, I am prepared to go gently into the night.

I am now a man of afflictions, derelictions, borne with diseases of unknown sorts, my sense of reality, aborts.

When weighed down by boulders of wrath, do not become too weak to pour miracles into your spirit.
Daily, seek to infuse spiritual waters into your soul, to wash away sediments of affliction, and seeds of discontent.

Spiritual embers within the soul, can become brush fires of faith to to torch thistles of trials and tribulations.

During fretful days of senility, struggling to stay upright, lean on Thy rod and staff.
If you should stumble and fall, may it be onto the bosom of our Lord and savior, Jesus Christ.
Do not allow aging frailties to compromise faith in Thee.

Use razors of faith to shave hairs of doubt, from your weary, but precious soul.
Undying will be my faith, when I come to Thee on bending knees, seeking relief from boughs of iniquity.

"SASA"

Subservient/Atonement/ Supreme Self Worth/Absolute
Pillars of faith during life struggles with good, bad and evil. .
Man does not not knoweth whether or not their God intervenes, monitors, everyday activities, only suspicions,
During latter stages of life, many days are fraught with swords of disappointment and despair,
A most worrisome downcast can be the inability to inspire off-springs to seek higher goals that lead to self- fulfillment.
Untimely deaths of siblings can wobble knees, evolving constant struggles to maintain beliefs in biblical teachings.

Idioms of SASA, have been, and continue to be, my bedrock during times of peril, as a worldwide pandemic has turned humanity inside out.
Imposed seclusion, lock- downs, have created islands of loneliness, like never before. But, life goes on, and we must adjust, or perish.
Being Subservient, seeking Atonement for sins of omission, while remaining "Absolute", regarding self – worth, are keys to help avoid deepened states of sadness, and calls for help, from outside sources.
Time waits for no one, and we all are culpable to fangs of mortality. These troubled times have provided serene moments, during which truth, consequence,have been put in proper perspective.
Seeking relief from fretful bouts with unrestrained anger, brought on by the sudden passing of beloved ones,., have led to re-examining long held opinions regarding the Almighty's role in deaths of mortals.

Life during the pandemic has been a struggle, in accepting the truth that we mortals are mere saplings, and our deaths have no ties to our Lord, and savior.
The saying, that this viral form of a holocaust was "God's will", has been flushed from my SASA well, freeing me of struggles with religion, its varieties, or lack thereof.
Thoughts, beliefs, regarding inequities of life, have been put on plates of "survival of the fittest," and ever present, Father Time.

During turbulent times, when "SASA" is up on trial, belief in my "Five Leaf Clover Scrolls", calm storms of discontent .

I have to look no further than the truths of "Circumstance, Clairvoyance, Coincidence, Destiny, Fate, each independent of the other, but yet no different in representation.

The art of being "Subservient", involves putting rights, wrongs, bitters, sweets, verities of life, in one's hip pocket, and accepting all holes that may proliferate.

Atonement, calls for one to flap wings of forgiveness, seeking relief from egregious sins of omission.

Attending church, religious chapels, not enough to cleanse the soul of hypocrisy wounds.

It takes time, commitment, to get the "burning feeling in the heart", which brings sheer joy to the soul.

One is born anew, fueled by infernal blessings rued from, blood, sweat, tears, pursuing things that really matter..

Such subservience frees one of guilt, setting the soul free to roam in search of "Self- Fulfillment.

". Self-Fulfillment", is a rather unique word, with numerous connotations. Can any mortal reach the apogee of quantum acceptance of self.

Tis might be impossible for any mortal to know what it takes to survive wiles of "Circumstance, eyes of Clairvoyance, uncertainties of Coincidence, slings, arrows, of Destiny, certainties of fate, .

Self- Fulfillment's uppermost limb, is the bough we all seek, .

Absolute, according to Webster's dictionary engulfs, "perfect, pure, unrestricted, ultimate/perfectly embodying the nature of a thing/unmitigated/free from imperfection.

Silence abounds in the world of "Absolutes", there are no echoes, nor walls from which souls can boomerang, leaving doubt, as the conundrum, mere mortals must navigate.

Many underprivileged, subservient people can offer that life's journey commenced with odds stacked against them via slavery.. This humanity curse oppressed millions of citizens of African descent, with nil punishments for the oppressor.

With my bent back, I sloshed through life on roller skates, always trying to balance tricky scales of the good, bad, ugly .Now that the end is near, I no longer worry about things I cannot control nor lack of flowers of success, I wear my "Five Leaf Clover Scrolls', as a pendant strung around my neck, to keep my soul in tune with "Silence of the Am"...

"LIFE'S BITS-N-PIECES"

I ain't what I used to be/But I am, who I am /No final decree/Still swinging, trying to hit life"s grand slam,
Still trying to rise up off, poverty's floor/Open success, steel door/Get rich/Strut, like an ostrich,

But, frail, worn is this body of mine/Voices of old age whine/Fast moving years entwine/I have slipped past da three threescore-and-ten timeline,

I see, I see/Floating images of da last bit-n -pieces of me"/Right before my dimming eyes/Wafting in 10,000 rainbow dyes/Body scales,, fly off into da mist/Feverishly, I try to stoke my bucket list,

I have reached the age of "Forgetting"/Dementia gods, are now doing da vetting/I have one foot in Alzymus tunnel/Da no return hole, shaped like an upside down funnel/Da darkened pit/Where da end of life, hounds sit/ In wait/For the sure to come ashes to ashes, dust to dust, human bait,

I am slowly drowning in my own tears./All the while, trying to duck mortality spears/Depression alley never clears/ It is home to da sum of all my fears,

Wait a minute, at seventy five years old/I ain't ready for my eyelids to fold/I have to be bold/Come in from da cold/Put hubris in my strut/ Go on a cabaret glut/Rid da soul of all mortality smut/Blow to smithereens, dementia's hut ,
Stop complaining 'about my wounded left knee/ Snap some fruit off the Liagara tree/To revive my hormone virility/ Jump start my now dormant powers of erectility/Here comes, innervated bits-n-pieces of me/I'm gonna make the rest of life, sweeter, than honey from a bee,

Tis way past time to crawl out of the septuagenarian hole/Where I now burrow, like a mole/As years, fly by faster than a weaver's shuttle/I have to find a rebuttal/Construct a quality over quantity, "Ambience Hut"/Make living a cabaret, before da doors of life, slam shut.

Life, you a "Karmapucka/All about, "I ain't yo sucka"/ Demands you must earn, what you get/Never known to vet,
Sir Life, I'm a misconception/A deception/
Human distortion /Who would have benefited greatly, from an abortion, Styopos, "Bits-n Pieces", not my thing /You have to throw it all, into da ring/I have no time to play/Say what you wanna say,
Well. no use lying, sinning/I absolutely, hate, I had a beginning/ My being born, your mistake/Life, you should have drowned me, in "Pregnancy's Lake/I often beg/Why me, in the chance union of sperm-n-egg/Zillions of sperm cells, were wiggling their tails/Spurred on by, orgasmic wails/ Why from that swarm, you chose to pluck/The wiggly one that yielded, Styopos J. Buck.

Look, Styopos J. Buck/I did not deliver you into this universal sphere/We haven't met, even after, you got here/You have a beef, seek out Lady Luck/ In your mind, go to the far reaches/Troll for yo "Bits-n-Pieces/I bet you will not find/ A single encounter, I have with mankind/I am a condition"/ For each mortal, a brief expedition/I distinguish/Father Time's angels, extinguish/I am the" HIgher Spirit's, connection to nature/I maintain mankind's existence/ Via da "Higher Spirit's assistance,

ANOTHER DAY

"Another Day"/Blown/Into da mist, flown/Never again to come my way, Squandered /As I idly wandered/Up and down Andy's Alley/Which is slowly becoming a mystic valley My mind rambles/Is tattered, in shambles/Due to da ageing process/As I continue to mentally regress,

Skidding thru da "Septo- Octo Gap"/Da ten year period in da lives of men, where da mind begins to unsnap/I shudder, when thoughts come of numerous days wasted/Without nary an apple seed of success tasted, Precious time, rolling into da mist/While I quibbled with my antiquated bucket list,

Which is now, a litany of unfulfilled dreams/No proverbial, peaches and creams, Time never stands still/Dumping hours into da run of da mill, As "Another Day" slips by,leaving nary a trace/I toss bricks at its ever changing face/ Wasted,/No success wind on my face, pasted, t,

" Another Day"/ A steep price, to pay/ For non-use/Abuse/ I've run out of excuses/I now cower to sounds from, "Beasts of Failure", muses,

I need to wake up, get off my ass/Tis time to play da long awaited round of golf, at CPC Rawgrass/Stop complaining 'bout aching knees/ Cursing da cost of green fees,

Have the moxie of my ninety year old next door neighbor/Start enjoying da fruits of my labor/ Like he says/With what you leave, someone else, plays, Tis way past time to stop dreaming/Start live streaming/No mas Allusions/ Illusions,

Cease being a discombobulated/Agitated/Elf/Cursing my temerity laden, self/Be happy always on da run/Chasing da west to east rising sun,

Need a spark/Wind my way down to R.O. Miller Park/Run in circles around one of its fabled "Pink Lamp Posts"/With gooses, goblins, my hosts, I keep tooting my Metal Pea whistle/My soul's inspiration thistle/Its sounds no one hears/Leads me to tears,

"Another Day"/Cannot afford to slay/I need to come in from da cold/ Before life wings fold,

Must infuse this fast decomposing body of mine/With some anti-ageing creams/Bathe in pierian water streams/To slow my fast decline,

No mo, feel sorry for self, blues/Time to slip on my SJB running shoes/ Strap on my red colored bandana/Run, run, listening to blares of "Oh Susanna",

Need the swagger of Casanova/Steely nerves, to survive a run with da bulls in Pamplona/In its hell on earth arena of fire/As I fulfill a lifelong desire,

Discovered an inspiring way/To maximize, "Another Day"/Journeyed to observe da return of swallows to San Juan Capistrano/Took along my treasured banjo/Had a wonderful time observing nature ebb and flow/ Da "Lady" put on quite a show,

Plucked my banjo animatedly, as hordes of Swallows landed atop da roof of a church's steeple/Amidst oohs, awes, from everyday people/ Da crowd cheered loudly/As I plucked my banjo, proudly,

Tis "Another Day" ,with hands on hip,I stare in my bathroom mirror/ Illusions, get clearer/Images of a horde of fast moving, bulls, appear/ Vivid, crystal clear/Poof, disappear//I shed a tear,

I've become obsessed/Possessed/With notions of running with da bulls in Pamplona/Along with sun bathing in Tuckson, Arizona, "Another Day"/ just slipped thru my fingers/Da agony lingers/Gone, into da mist/As I tinker with my "Bucket List',

Move "Run with Bulls, to the top/Will not flip flop/Running out of time, no pun, intended/Each upcoming day, will be hyperextended,

Tis near,,closure of the "Septo-Octo Gap"/ Brain cells have begun to un-snap/Have to fight mightily not to spend "Another Day" in a daze/ Delusional, akin to a rat in a maze,

No mo dreaming/All things now, live streaming/Time is of the essence/ In day to day battles with senescence,

No mas, "Another Day", muddling/'Septo-Octo Gap, befuddling/ Procrastination/ All, soul, spirit elevation,

. "Another Day"/With which to parlay/Bets, $100,000, Tiger next major, Cowboys over Rams/Dey better be slams,

To all fellow septuagenarians, future "Octos", out there, shed all da sloth chaff off yo noses, smell da roses, enjoy da succulent fruits of yo labor, buy yourself a Rolls Royce like my ninety six year old neighbor.

"Another Day"/Time slot/That is all you got/Father Time will, eventually, check slay.

I GOT TODAY UNDER MY SKIN

I have "Today", under my skin/Filled with anti- ageing melanin/Gotta live it as though it's my last/Bury all sordid remnants of da past, Roll da dice/Trust da west to east sun to set twice/,
Kiss da face of "Today"/ Imbibe each sunray/Let nary a second go unused/ Be abused,
I Invert my "Sourglass"/Revert rate at which sans pass/Choose quality/ Over quantity/ Ride da Choo Choo Trains of ambience/ Expedience/ Revelry/Chivalry.

Infuse da soul with pellets of spontaneity/Rid life of each complexity/ Freelance/Revel in happenstance/Fill da time cup with forever young, substance/Glance/Use powers of clairvoyance/Take a stance/Peek into da ever changing world of romance/, Go on a cabaret glut run/Chasing da west to east setting sun,
Today, you a "Twoday/ Match da "beauty, flair of my gal, Rene/Oh happy "Today", oh happy "Today"/Sure wish forever, you could stay.

GET "TUMORROW" FROM UNDER MY SKIN

Have to prevent thoughts of "Tumorrow" from burrowing under my skin/Gobbles up melanin/Casts eerie shadows on "Today"/On it, bets, one cannot parlay,
Father Time/For every reason, rime/You can shelter "Tumorrow"/Unless from it, I can borrow/ A few hours of daylight/All sunny, bright/Allowing me to golf six extra rounds/Afterwards, clear my psyche, via my "Metal Pea", whistle sounds.
"Tumorrow", you are one of a kind nomadic metaphor/ You are akin to a quadrupedal stegosaurus dinosaur/Your face never appears/But, you hold da sum of all fears.

"YESTIDDY"

"Yestiddy", to you I acquiesce. You play by your own rules, your rascality is legendary. Once you gone, you gone, with no passage way of return. So, to you I doff my "SJB" cap, never try to awaken you from your nap. Yestiddy/Though closure liddy/During its twenty four hours time slot,, we be giddy/Lovingly kiss a face, that is ever so"priddy/But, once it's gone, it's gone/Into da past, alone/Never to return/It's wheels of time, no longer, churn.'.

RIPPLES IN DA STREAM

Shadowy, Ripples in da Streams"/Mystic waters into which I have dumped buckets of shattered dreams/Sadly, watch them float away from shore/A scene I've witnessed many times before/While sitting atop the hood of my 1956 Chevy/Parked on Oppaloosa Levee.

Murky ripples proliferate/As I meditate/Trying mightily to understand why a single dream did not come to fruition/All perishing like pulp fiction/As listless tides flow downstream/Flushing away dream after dream,
During my treasured moments of meditation/Reflecting on dreams that came true/Such as the one whereby I reunited with long since departed, Uncle Hue/From out of the blue, dream fragments placed the two of us in a bright red canoe/Snagging red horse fishes/Smacking our lips in anticipation of having a fill of Mama's fried fish dishes,

On this bright, sunny day/Ripples criss-cross amidst blinding sunlight/All types of flickering rainbows come into play/What an awesome sight, Misting rain, glancing off sun rays/Intermingle light with ripples in da stream/I let off steam//Reflect back on all the good times during my hey days/Those days of wine and roses/ Super will imposes/When I didn't need no dream/I was da ripple in da stream,
But Father Time don;t know nothing about no dream/Its peaches or cream/No dream creator/It's obliterator,

I toss my empty dream bucket/Onto the bed of my 56 Chevy/Point it towards the road back to Nantucket/Blow a kiss at beloved Oppaloosa Levee Can hardly wait to get back to Nantucket's Samojo Beach/Walk barefoot in its silted sands mirroring colors of a rotten peach/Yoga, wiggle my toes/In da sand, relieve shattered dream woes/Watch as white doves land/On the Strand/I have so named "Devil's Bow"/Home to my favorite pot bellied rainbow.. Dream,dream.

"SEVEN-SEVEN-EIGHT-O"

You have to live it, to no so/All mortality demons awaken between ages "Seven–Seven", and "Eight–O.
Octogenarians offer that the time period is also one, in which mortality demons don nightgowns, and become full- fledged, changeling clowns,

I just hit the "Seven-Seven " spot, in da "Septo –Octo Gap", and you can best believe life patterns have begun to unravel, unsnap.
Thought patterns are dire, faceted with urgency and reality bites, aplenty. I ain't got much time left on Mother Earth, no matter how many times I spin da wheels of time. Everywhere I twist, turn, all I encounter are witches of age, mortality clowns, robed in purple nightgowns,
."Eight-O", many folks do not reach the ominous demarcation line between life/ death. Irrationality of aging lies within the zone of one rejecting visual proof of physical, mental decline,
We do not look like we think we do, if you get what I mean. In my case, I don't visualize much difference between ages fifty and "Seven-Seven", except for a few gray hairs, here and there. My life patterns hadn't changed much, until ghosts of "Eight-O '' appeared in my rear view mirror.

Currently, a time warp entwines days, months, years at dizzying speeds, coming down da pike akin to a runaway choo choo train.
I try to fight back the years to no avail,
Perplexing thoughts of mortality, make shallow, once overflowing rivers of life. Friends are few, so are things not already seen, heard or experienced. So, what is one left with? I will put it succinctly, the power of the will to keep on pushing, no matter the odds lying on the actuarial table of truths. We can't be afraid of dying,

Though departure is inevitable, we tend to feel that it applies to the other person. Well, wait until you reach age "seven-seven", you will quickly realize, you are now the other person. Attendance in church, rounds of golf, casino excursions, cruises etc., define many aged folks calendars late in life.

Raising the interest level in any endeavor, takes a whole lot of prodding. There is very little to lean on for many aged ones as they tumble through the "Septo-Octo Gap",.

"Eight-O" is on the horizon, and I have to accept my inevitable date with demons of mortality. Oh,how sad the hour will be, when selected from all the wasted years. Folks keep saying "Eight-O", is just a number, but that is not giving the most ominous in a lifespan, It's due. If I am lucky enough to reach the milestone, you can bet your bottom dollar I will have finished my obituary, cast aside all seeds of immortality, and try to live each remaining day twice. There shall be no more distinction between days of the week. The habit of waiting for the weekend is to be no more.

To all you younger folks out there, a life span is a mere whisper in time. An individual person is akin to a grain of sand on a deserted beach.
Two days out of each remaining week, I shall not change clothes, will not undress, only to redress six hours later.
What "karmapucking" difference does it make, whether or not I throw on a pair of pajamas or sleep in my Kevi Red jeans? Ain't it all just a routine carried out by mortals day in and day out.
You figure, how many days do you think are lost during a lifespan, following normalized routines.
After one reaches a certain age, the amount of sleep required to survive, usurps time like a drunkard downing a bottle of whiskey.
Sleep gobbles up a lot of time but you can't have one without the other.. With squalls of Covid-19 consuming breathable air, nighttime hours might just be the safest. Covid has burned five, six years of what would have been a key productive cycle of time for many aged ones. y Get all material things you covet, divest of all things hoarded, advice given to we aged ones, but hard to goodwill..

Ain't no use in saving anything anymore. Got to break ninety in golf otherwise I may as well toss all clubs into Chavez Ravine. All books shall be completed. Close the door on Infidelity's angels, they no longer care about me, no use caring about them.
Gotta be pure in mind , body, soul, acclivity, and treat each day as though it's my last.

MAN OF AGE

My face, once smooth as da butt of a newborn nursling babe, now, has lines, and more lines, mirroring those in a dilapidated tin roof.
Lines proliferate, as my face continues to degenerate into folds, solid as frozen leather. My "floater" diffused eyes, create distortions, as my sight fades from light to dark shadowing everything in between.

Neck muscles have lost elasticity and bulge favoring organ pipes. Muscles, nerves, in erotic tissues, no tenacity, to ignite flames of sexual desire,
Da skin on my arms, chest, abdominal area, are flushed with purplish spots, labeled," mortality dots. A receding hairline,have turned the anterior of my head, into a V-shaped façade. Bones in knees, ankles, shoulders, hip joints, ache, incessantly.
I find myself grasping for straws, while being strangled by Father Time paws, sitting astride life's veritable see-saw, frosted hair will not thaw. My back is bent, lurching me forward, like my ninety six year old Uncle Joe, as I stumble down life's winding road to nowhere..
My feet ache, swell, get puffy, akin to a ripened cotton boll. Varicose veins proliferate, bringing forth shortness of breath, that often leave me gasping for air, like those struck by a Covid-19 blow. .
My ears ring, mirroring at times, sounds of 10,000 crickets.. in Tinnitus, thickets,
Staying mentally alert,is a day by day thing.., win . lose, draw.. Though time is no longer on my side, I still have my pride, zest for life.
"Have to bust out of "Moe Tallurty's" cage?/ Become the long awaited, prolific clown of renown, before exiting life's stage,
I can't stop "Da Drain"/ Fast, fast, drips my dementing brain / Emptying akin to speed of a lightning flash,/Into insanity's darkened hole, I dash.
Alzymus gods/ Violently rattle my sanity pods/Crush my brain stem / Fuel insanity mayhem/
Alzy,why do me po,/I've just reached the ripe old age of seventy- fo/ Da age of reason/ Not treason./ I ain't putting my left foot in yo tunnel/Da hole rumored to be shaped like an upside down funnel/ Word has it as

being a darkened abyss/Where dementia demons hiss//Da brain begins to burn/ Said to be da pit of no return,

I have got to stop "Da Drain"/Warped is my fast deteriorating brain/ Got me running backwards in time/ Mortality bells have begun to chime, No, no, Knowus, I do not wish to ride on yo back to da past, boat/ Dis "Man of Age", wanna ride on da into da future float,

To preview, Heaven, Hell, Purgatory /Befo I decide, which will be my ashes to ashes, dust to dust, depository,

I have to stop "Da Drain"/Re- fertile my brain/Using apple seeds/Soaked in juices of milkweeds/Stymie da dementia gods /Fiddling with my memory pods,

Dis "Man of Age"/Has got to find means to enjoy life's final stage/ Yesterday,I peeked into Alzymus tunnel/True, tis shaped like an upside down funnel /I recoiled, deafened by whistling sounds, akin to those of my metal pea/ Caught a glimpse of cauldrons of ashes, being washed out to sea.

Da sighting, rolled me into panic mode/Spent some time in a fitness center sauna/Replenished my brain's mother lode/Ain't ready to feed " da fauna", But, I now understand/As a " Man of Age" /Tis a must, to survive in "La la land"/During life's final stage./ Have to be my own time czar/Brain drain, stopper/Sanity hopper/Bought myself a new, ZMW car.

"WE COME AND GO"

In our prayers of introspect, retrospect, let us not be circumspect, in our honesty, about life's travails.
"We Come And GO", up and down roads more traveled than the 405 Freeway in da City of Angels.
As we age, are we able to pass each other in da streets of life, free of flashing glares of contempt,, as we struggle with demons of anonymity.
We must be astutely aware that "racism" is not a proxy giving inalienable rights to judge others according to race, color or creed. Racism is a double edged sword and cuts deep into the fabric of civilization. We often become a bit overzealous in judging neighbors due to unfound rumors that travel like wildfire,

"We Come And Go", individually, in masses, all part of life's ebb and flow. through epidemics, pandemics, wars, deaths,
We brought nothing into this fast moving world, and most certainly will not take anything with us. But opportunities abound to make the world a better place to live, if we have the zeal to do so.
History is earmarked by individuals who sought to go the extra mile.

Nevertheless, death is a formidable force that runs outside the control of mankind and wields its own scythe.
Individuals are mere sans in an hourglass, but are blessed with superior intelligence which sets them apart from lower forms of life.
A life span, when taken in context to ages of the sun, moon, stars, oceans, pales in comparison.
Tis a chilling fact,no one lives forever. Father Time is a silent assassin and grows more ominous as we age which causes many of us to panic.
We try to be young all over again but end up at the short end of the stick for not accepting the fact that Father Time is undefeated..
There is no distinction, when it comes to human extinction. Lay down your arms if you have entered the "Septo-Octo Gap" and try like heck to not get sucked into" Alzymus Tunnel, home of Dementia mules. As far as Father Time goes, a human biped suffers the same fate as a Pangolin, Aardvark.. snail , octopus., elephant, shark. mosquito..

"POTPOURRI MIND SLAKE"

Styopos, you come up with names, titles, that distort the English language. This title, Potpourri Mind Slake", takes the proverbial cake, as the saying goes..

It all depends on what kind of cake you are talking about, Brother Eli. Cakes come with different tastes, shapes, toppings, ingredients, names, sizes. So "Potpourri Mind Slake", is not that rare, when you put things in proper perspective. It simply contains ingredients such as " metaphors, similes, allegories, that seek to nourish da imagination, sliding back and forth between real, unreal, sanity, insanity.

"Potpourri Mind Slakes" yield narratives that seek to push one's imagination to its outermost limit, while at the same time, maintaining simplicity in nature.

Metaphors, allegories, similes provide means to express lifelong disgruntlement, against perceived evils of slavery, poverty, or everyday mundane existence..
So don't tell me you haven't been a Potpourri Mind Slaker ", at some point in your life.

Mortals all around the world,espouse the belief that the gift of imagination plays a huge role in defining the character of humans, pushing them to a higher mental plateau... This belief flourishes when one picks up a writing pen and imagination becomes its inkwell.

Imagination allows one to experience, uncover, wonders of life, far beyond those privy to lesser forms of animal species, of which there are multitudes. Just as "potpourri" requires a conglomeration of leaves, peelings,flowers, from plants, to foment its characteristic scents, the same holds true for the human mind.

Time is a terrible thing to waste, and affects the briefness of a human life span. My mind is constantly in motion "Potpourri Slaking", as I fight da witches of old age, nipping at my heels.

I have been a "time mongerer", strapped to a sixty year old cotton sack,, filled to the brim with bolls that are forever rotting.

Stench of poverty, is near the top of my potpourri 's list of putrid scents. Along da way I have tossed in orange, lemon, peelings, to abate its odours, but to no avail.
Egregious failures add putrid scents to life's potpourri flower vases. Matching words to rumblings of the mind can be a bit challenging to both novice and seasoned literary provocateurs.

Psychology pig stys are stacked with books, pamphlets, drafts, which attempt to unlock potpourri slaking of both brilliant and demented minds, Tis through imagination fields, that our minds are able to use scents of sanity to ward off dementia dragons of insanity.. In order to navigate mine fields of metaphors, twisted allegories, stunted similes, the brain uses its network of nerve ganglia to lay bare what is scented. Provident beings use imagination sparkles, that are as illuminating as shinings from the Milky Way, to create such as the magical world of Disney..
Then there are those of us, who misuse imagination sparkles, to wreak havoc on society via . mass killings, rioting, gang wars.
The point I am trying to make is one which illustrates that "Potpourri Mind Slaking", sets us apart from lower forms of animal species.

There is a plethora of putrid, potpourri scents that splatter throughout human life spans, which leave lasting odors in our wake.
Nauseating scents dripping from low self- esteem gutters, lead da pack. I dare not mention adverse peelings, of the id, ego, superego, potpourri clambakes to the highest degree.

The Sars virus could continue to mutate, and evolve as da greatest Potpourri Mind Slaker", in the history of mankind. It is unrivaled in its plurality, devastation.

Potpourri Mind Slake", good for the soul. Follow life's scents, devour" Potpourri Slakes", along da way.

LEETHA KOVID

"Leetha Kovid.", struck close to home again/Laid my soul bare, with pain/ In da nude, I run circles in pouring rain/That's flooding "Mortality' Plain,, Which is a huge, desert like landfill/Flush with decaying bodies, headstones, tattered flower baskets/Silhouetted, by an array of molded caskets,
Into a big, black hole, decomposing ruins, spill. I awaken in a cold sweat/ Fully aware that "Leetha"" is breathing down my neck/Is an accursed threat/I shudder at prospects of becoming a mortality speck, As if being led/I take to turning back flips, atop my bed/Screaming, ", Leetha I ain't dying/ My ass, you ain't, karmapucking frying/In yo Sars pan/Infect me, if you can".
"Leetha", as a bonafide, nomadic metaphor, you smothering relatives, friends, like it's a walk in da park/In broad daylight, in da dark/ Is da coronavirus, yo lightning spark/ Or mortality bark...
Leetha, you in a metaphor world of your own, fortified by da following beauties, "da nostril splitter, viral home run hitter,da scavenger with coyote fangs., da wind of destruction, da viral incinerator, even though you are invisible to da naked eye.".
Truthfully, no collection of words can capture, nor describe the destruction, carnage, of human souls.
Leetha, I hear you have a mutant brother virus, that you "strained'. What, you viral devils, wish to sweep Mother Earth clean of all inhabitants, leaving da gate open for a showdown between you and "Soggyhawk Bakkteria, your rival.
No matter you two body invaders., degraders, wont' ever outpace the process of procreation, too many wiggly sperm cells searching for aa home..
Styopos J, Buck,/ Da Lord speaking, quit worrying 'bout Leetha Kovid/On it put a lid/ Trust yo "vaccine shinings/ Gather all medical silver linings./ You better grab da hand of Lady Luck,
Your sense of survival, trust//Pray like hell, you avoid, ashes to ashes, dust to dust,
The onslaught of carnage, that's now pillaging relatives, friends, is mind boggling..

In remorse, Leetha, Iuse to say you were just a plain ol nomadic metaphor. The sam as some of my favorite sayings, "I love the smell of life", "the bases are empty, as a school room in August", "Cane River, was my mirror", "my putter, is now cold as ice", but now I acquiesce, you win. You a bad karmapucka.

I will just have to live with the perception that you, "Leetha Kovid, is one of the three heads of Lucifer, gather souls for the Inferno, as a snowflake from hell, toting a pitchfork. Get on, with yo bad, karmapucking self, you are the sky without stars, ocean minus water, fire minus heat..

Lucifer, hell, Hurricane Katrina, wildfires, tsunamis, all rolled into one. Devil, or witch, whichever you are/No matter, God remains the universes CZAR/Leetha Kovid- !9/You ain't no match for da Almighty's spirit laden Vaccine.

"MODIMI"
MUSE, OPTIMIST, DILETTANTE, ICONOCLAST, MARTYR, ICON

"Modimi", gracias, fer da "walk da precipice", escapade, monitored by Muse. It christened my being an eternal "Optimist," and pushed me to become a "Dilettante" of existential arts.

After the "Precipice", an exhilarating dream, infused my "Iconoclastic" nature. I became a "Martyr", in my own mind, elevating me to "Icon" status. As an eternal "Optimist", I shall "walk da precipice of greatness", with hubris when in need and, light fuses of MODIMI, to enlighten da path to existential joy, as a "Dilettante", supreme.

"MODIMI", drips from felt marker pen during my obsession with creating a palette masterpiece of myself.

When that MODIMI mountain is scaled, I will self induct into the rarefied air of "Martyrs".

I fully realize that it takes more than wishful thinking, to become a "Dilettante", extraordinaire, of the arts, but my drive to become an "Iconoclastic, Icon", along with "MODIMI", will allow me to probe the existential edge of intelligence, in search of "Dilettante Martyrdom". Iconoclast seeds, in my soul, have sprouted "Muse" fruits in a prolific manner so I proudly deem myself an "Icon"...

"Da claws of mediocrity/ Ain't no match, for Da paws of "MODIMI", Rush on.

If you do not understand MODIMI, tis okay, I don't either. Its leaves sprouted during the rarefied air of an epileptic seizure.

ACROSS DA GREAT BEYOND

Across Da Great Beyond/Every mortal will take flight/Where ripples afterlife's "Golden Pond"/Matters not, day or night,
Golden Pond, epitome of beauty/ Serene, tranquility/ Upon departure from earth's surly grounds/Across the astral plane where existential beauty abounds,

A life span is much like blowing out a candle wick, with one breath of air/Void of any tinge of flair/. We are here today, gone tomorrow/Leaving behind trails of happiness, sorrow,

Only the departed knows what lies/, "Across da Great Beyond"/Experiences da warmth, coldness, of waters in eternity's Golden Pond /In which one's spirit, never drowns, or dies,

But, we shouldn't mind, because our destinies rarely stray far from our beliefs, and imprints we leave behind.
We plant,, water, fertilize our trees of life and what groweth on each limb, depends solely upon what we poureth into life's soils.

As we age/There is no need to whine/No one escapes mortality's rage/Nor efface its drawn in and, timeline.

Our graying hairs can be hidden, shaved away/ But nothing silences da sounds of Father Time's flute/ It's sounds, all the king's men, horses, cannot mute/To life's pied piper, all mortals pay.

I admit/As we age/We carry within, a silent rage/ That eats away at the stomach pit,

But, there is no basis to whine/If fortunate enough to cross da threescore-and-ten timeline/All years beyond/Make them your earth's "Golden Pond",

No matter da race, color, pedigree/From mortality's claws/Paws/ Nary an animal species springs free/We are all radicals of time dispersions/Return to fauna, conversions,

Across da Great Beyond/Lies mankind's Golden Pond/ Spirits fly away to its shore/Where await surreal scenes, never witnessed before//Trust your imagination/ To be the pilot in your navigation/Flap your angelic wings to create your own wind swept current//To flight da astral plane during ascentEach mortal will fly away alone/That truth is set in stone/When from the surly bounds of earth we flee/To the shore where da soul, from flesh, apogee,
Life's elixir, my fertile imagination /From whence its roots came came, only God knows/The power of its existentialism in my soul flows/There is no end to its elevation,
My mortality clock has stuck eleven/Swing open da gates to heaven/ No tears/Just have to bear, da sum of all fears,

We all will have our sightings/During flightings/Across da Great Beyond/ They will sustain us, as we walk da shores of eternity's Golden Pond,
My sojourn on earth, hasn't been much/Just a stack of rubble of, such and such/At life norms, never had a chance/Due to the wiles of circumstance,
When I fly Across da Great Beyond/I hope to see da "Light"/ That sanctifies every heavenly flight/To where sits, eternity's "Golden Pond",

Use just your imagination/Void of aberration/Triumph your flight across Da Great Beyond/Bathe in heaven's/Golden Pond/Cleanse your being of all earthly sins/Tis surreal, where da afterlife, begins, Ping, ping, ping/ Tis time to awaken from your, virtuality sting/Left no live streams/Tis metaphor induced but the 'Great Beyond" infiltrate dreams,
Via Ecclesiastic's Lane/Just above the astral plane/Each mortal's soul will spiral **"Across da Great Beyond"/Onto the shores of Heaven's, Golden Pond.**

FIVE LEAF CLOVER SCROLLS

For any mention of a Five Leaf Clover, tis natural to assume such exists somewhere on planet earth and is an offshoot of normal , three leaf ones. But, not so quick. A five leaf clover is a rare breed with only three ever witnessed over the landscape of the entire universe,
An image of a five leaf clover sprung, from after effects, of a traumatic grand mal seizure, and led to a surreal excursion to gain possession of one of the majestic marvels.
From deep within the twilight zone of an epileptic seizure, flashed images of a "Five Leaf Clover", which glistened amidst a patch of clover emitting vermilion colored light, chameleonic in nature, at times.
As I drifted in and out of consciousness, images of the clover stuck in the far reaches of my brain.

A few nights later, another dream fomented, curtailing into my being wrapped in an old quilt, adorned with patches of clover, with one distancing itself from all others.
The dream revealed my being fascinated with a unique feature that was rather unique: the clover pulsated, similar to a "Firefox". A fungal type plant, A voice in my head kept whispering," you are to guide your remaining days on earth according to wiles, past, present future of Circumstance, Clairvoyance, Coincidence(Lady Luck), Destiny, Fate. These five entities are adjudicated to be your da "Five Leaf Clover Scrolls".
I was haunted by constant resonations from the unknown voice akin to sounds of a flute.
Sure enough another, lucid dream followed, revealing the "Five Leaf Clover", with each leaf, scripted with a word, barely legible, in bits, pieces. During the dream, from out of the shadows, came a figure adorned in jeans, sandals, quilted like shirt, sombrero eyes emblazoned.
The shadow of a man-like figure bore around its neck. A glistening necklace, bearing a five leaf clover. Due to surrealistic light, I could barely discern the letters on each leaf.
Struggling mightily, I deciphered the following, Circumstania, Clairvoyasa, Luckasa, Destinata, Fatesia.

Upon awakening, from the grand mal induced dream, sightings of the shadowy figure, necklace, continued to haunt me. Forever smitten, by surrealism, realism, of the dream, I took it upon myself to bring meaning to the mystic driven experience.

So for some reason or another, the name , Styopos J. Buck, resonated amidst flute sounds and I circumscribed the five words into. Circumstance, Clairvoyance, Luck, Destiny, Fate, as fore played by the unknown voice in my head. "Five Leaf Clover Scrolls", my tentacles of truths and consequences.

Similar dreams that followed, linked the scrolls to my long since dead, Uncle Hue, and discovery of a live "Five Leaf Clover" on the Cliffs of Poezydun, in a remote region of Acadover, Dellyware.

"Homings" of life truths, consequences, "Comings" of the "Five Leaf Clover Scrolls. my dyed in wool, proven proverbs of life are woven from threads of Circumstance,Clairvoyance, Lady Luck, Destiny, Fate, I can't get around them, and cower beneath their tenets of power.

The arms of "Circumstance", dumped me into this cosmos,, and most surely will take me out. I always wonder, what would 've had occurred,if my father had bedded down one minute earlier, on that starry night in February, when I was conceived. Would there even be a Styopos J, Buck, I doubt it seriously.

We all must have guard rails in life, to keep us on a straight and narrow path. Oftentimes we have to add a few ounces of fantasy, to our cups of reality, to get a full picture of life's true meaning. We all know life is a temporary fling, but we choose to live in a fantasy world of immortality. My sojourn on earth has been bittersweet. Nothing is sweeter than having the honor of being a child of one of the most special human beings ever created, my mother.

On the other hand, my deep seated hatred of oppression of the underclass, can't be matched in bitterness,

The conglomeration of sins committed against the underclass,. poor health care, housing, racial discrimination, lack of educational opportunities, drips with vinegar,

Looking back over the years, I can readily trace my jagged past, how my dye was cast, and the deleterious nature of fears, self imposed hatred,
Self hatred has nailed me to a cross, and my mind has been warped by the crude belief, that I never should have been conceived.
I have had a litany of nightmares about the timing of sperm +egg, on the fateful night, February, 1942, of conception.
Why didn't the karmapucking sperm that bombed da egg, leading to my conception, veer left, or, right, there would not be me,

Some nights it seems as though the Scrolls convene and I become a victim of their circular firing squad.
Tonight has been a restless one, hot, calciferous,, fraught with lamentations, as I wrestle with "Breasts of Failure", while ducking bullets fired at my shoulders, arms, knees, feet, hands by Destiny, Circumstance, with Clairvoyance screaming, "No mas golf, Styopos J. Buck".
My navel hurts, as my jaws tighten, when thoughts of truths about the wheels of time knock me off my feet.

Mockingly, I cock my head from side to side, envisioning all the sad times I had, when people laughed and called me "Jug Head".
After sixty-five years of denial, I acquiesce, have a big head, flat in the rear, but such allows my headgear to fit rather nicely,
Rumblings of Circumstance, Destiny, ring loud and clear, from time to time.. Circumstance, loves to needle by whispering, "I am da sperm, that hit yo mama's egg, dead center, no chance of another being, but you..Be glad you had a chance to experience life and all its travails..
Destiny intones, at times, "Styopos J. Buck", you were doomed the moment they laid your ass on the operating table, at Huey P. Wrong Hospital, Pineville, Looezyanna,

My soul is on fire, in the wee hours of the morning, furiously, I try to punch holes in da dark.
Dancing, prancing, skipping, imitating my Uncle Ted, who dreamed of becoming lightweight champion of da world.
My sanity is up on trial, as I pick up my seven iron golf club, swing it a zillion times, until I drop to my knees, fully exhausted.

I crawl over to a nearby wall, expectorate lucid mucus, use it to scribble a five leaf clover, attach the words Circumstance, Clairvoyance, Lady Luck, Destiny, Fate, to each imaginary leaflet.
I can always lean on their impositions, declarations, to ease my troubled mind,

I crawl under my bed, vow to remain there for "17" days, void of food, or any other type of supplication. I am going to hide from "Self, with hopes of scraping all chaff from my fast decomposing brain.
I fore go tampering with. the physical body, It is set in stone, If I can keep my mind, imagination, fertile, I stand a chance to resurrect my soul. and weave a few threads on mankind's legacy quilt.. I am going to sleep now, "Da Scrolls", will pull wool over my eyes..

IDIOMS OF STYOPOS J. BUCK

Styopos, can't you hear the wheels of time spin, you are now an aged lynchpin.

Shadows of life/death have begun to interlope/ Reflecting images of mortality's rope/I can no longer cope/Long gone, all threads of hope.

At my advanced age, each day turns its own page.

Aardvark feet, always first in alphabet soup.

I am yet to collect my bet from Peter Scruff,ante, a thousand to one,I favored Powder, over Puff..

Growing old gracefully, not for me, prefers immortality.

What am I living for, if not for me.

Anyone who claims no fear of dying, has no fear of lying.

Upon crossing the threshold of da "Threescore- n- ten", timeline, about age, no need to opine.

I can no longer fool myself, I have become a septuagenarian elf.

Island in da sun, lies inside da corona where fire gods run, crisscrosses da astral plane, that leads to "Lucifer Lane".

Tonight, I have a down home blues, dancing in da dark, clicking da heels of my blue suede shoes, moving like a hungry shark.

At my advanced age, always the oldest hamster in da cage,I am entitled to rage,

Sad, can no longer digest what I love to ingest, pork rinds and Aardvark soup.

Why do you keep," Circling da circle", aged fool/That surrounds life's drowning pool/ Into its waters, an octogenarian friend, slipped and fell/ Swore, there can't be any hotter pits in hell.

Imagination, da only source of reincarnation.. undisputed truth, bet you a Baby Ruth.

Grandpa, I will swallow yo old pipe, before I let you force me to eat cold tripe

I have absolutely no hunger for chitterlings.

I thought old age would be fun, even engage my honey bun, instead mortality's hounds keep me on da run, towards da west to east, setting sun.

Father Time has eroded all calculus nerves,within my demented brain.

DOGGERELS

Jump over da proverbial rainbow/Astride a witch's broom/With all shattered dreams in tow/Toss dem towards da heavens, hope like hell they bloom.

Father Time obliterates life spans, at an alarming rate/Everything that breathes, is on its slate/Vagabonds, kings, mules, whales, meadow Larks/Dang, how could it not include Aardvarks.

Sad, sad, is da sight of da old man/Kneeling on a street corner/Flashing a rusted tin pan/Falsifying need for aid for "Lil Jack Horner".

I prefer pure visages/They extend a bit longer than mirages.

Jealousy is the ever widening grave of hypocrisy.

Pitter patter, pitter patter/Broken hearts create a whole lot of chatter.

Once one crosses a three score and ten timeline/Mortality dye is cast/Months, years, entwine/We can be seen running from da past.

When we grow old/Life's curtains begin to fold/Mortality's bells begin to ring/We become mere puppets on a string.

Realized my worst of fears/Witnessed my beloved brother's death/I now drown in my own tears/With his passing went my last meaningful breath.

An epileptic spasm, leaves behind a lasting memory of da ominous, "life/death chasm.

My life span slipped right through my fingers, I leave behind, no legacy deadringers.

Boy, oh boy/At my septuagenarian life stage/When the angels scream, "ship ahoy"/I am akin to a rabid dog, let out of its cage.

www.ingramcontent.com/pod-product-compliance
Lightning Source LLC
LaVergne TN
LVHW061556070526
838199LV00077B/7076